JOURNEY
OF THE
ANGELS

Tobias

through
Geoffrey and Linda Hoppe

JOURNEY OF THE ANGELS

CRIMSON CIRCLE

Published by Crimson Circle Press,
a division of the Crimson Circle Energy Company, Inc.
PO Box 7394
Golden, Colorado USA
Contact: customerservice@crimsoncircle.com
Web: www.crimsoncircle.com

ISBN 9781712672990

Second Printing, January 2020

Printed in the United States of America

Cover Design: Geoffrey Hoppe
Book Design and Layout: Geoffrey Hoppe and Jean Tinder
Transcription: Gail Neube
Editing and Proofing: Jean Tinder

This is the story of creation that's never been told before, shared with us now by a real angel. It explains how and why we became separated from Spirit, helps us understand what transpires in the angelic realms, and paints a new and refreshing picture of why earth was created and why we chose to come here.

Journey of the Angels *is a spiritual epic. It's the explanation and understanding of creation from A to Z, allowing the reader to actually re-experience their own personal journey of existence and what it means going forward.*

This beautiful story is essential for anyone who wants to understand their human and angelic origins. At times it will challenge you, as well as give you great comfort and remembrance. You might be moved to tears or laughter as the Journey of the Angels *helps you remember.*

JOURNEY OF THE ANGELS

Content

AUTHOR'S NOTE

This is *your* story. As such, it may trigger deep feelings and reactions as the most ancient parts of you begin to awaken and remember. You are encouraged to give yourself the time and space to deeply feel each part of the journey as it unfolds.

This material was originally presented as a three-day workshop, with the opportunity for audience discussion and sharing after each session. This sharing assisted in grounding and integrating the experience. Therefore, you will find space at the end of each chapter where you can write down notes, thoughts and feelings.

Ask yourself, What am I feeling now? What do I especially want to remember? What does this part of the story mean to me? Give yourself the gift of these reflections as you revisit some of the most profound experiences you have ever had – as a human *or* an angel.

Chapter 1

All That Was

And so it is, dear human, dear angel, that we begin. Take a deep breath as we embark on a journey to understand how we got here. Together we will go back into All That Was, back to the very, very beginning in order to understand the journey of the angels, the experiences that we've had, the inner look at our soul and the outer expression of our self, in order to understand what has brought us to this point.

Why Remember?

As we embark on this journey, it is not about going back in time, because there actually is none, and it is not about going back to figure out all of the details about the past. Rather, it is about understanding where we have come from and why this time on Earth is so important. When you understand why you have chosen the experiences that you have chosen, why you have gone through the situations, challenges and joys that you have gone through, then you can go forward into the new times and into the realization of your Self as an expression of Spirit. You can go forward in your life free of karma, free of destiny, and free of the path that has brought you here, for today you begin a new awakening.

Today you can awaken to the realization that Spirit has always been within, and that there is no line separating you from Spirit or from your angelic roots. There is no obstacle course you must get through. There is no test that you have to take. There is only a choice to make: Are you ready to move into your full expression, into the I Am-ness of your being? Are you ready to get off of the path of the past in order to go into a future that can be anything you choose to create? For it is said that the future is the past healed.

In this new awakening, your tomorrow is the understanding and acceptance of everything that has come in all of your yesterdays. From this moment on, your choices can come from your heart and soul, instead of having to make amends for your past and fearing who you really are. Your choices no longer come having to remedy something that happened in the past, for now you can come to the acceptance of all that you have been and all that you are, in order to move forward into your full realization of Self.

Beginning the Journey

As this journey begins, understand that there are guiding angelic beings who are with you every step of the way. The message of this book, and the consciousness within the message, is coming from yourself, as well as from Tobias of the Crimson Council, and it will be as clear to you now as the day it was first presented. In this journey that will bring us from Home all the way to your present moment, we invite you to open your heart. We invite you to open to the true soul level, because your soul already knows this material. It may know it in a different form and different words, but your essence already understands.

We're going to ask you to step aside from the mind as you read, in order to allow your heart, your soul, the expression of the God within you to come forward. We invite you to allow yourself to remember, and to accept and love yourself during this entire journey.

We're going to tell this as a story, not to be taken literally but as a way to understand the energies, so that when we talk about Spirit you understand and feel the essence. When we talk about Mother-Father God, we invite you to feel the combination of the masculine and feminine energies coming together in wholeness and oneness. When we talk about the King and the Queen, these are metaphors for the masculine and feminine within, but they are also metaphors for the royalty that you are and always have been.

We're going to write in metaphors and stories, but beyond the words that we share, allow yourself to resonate with the essence.

Take a deep breath now and remember the Is-ness.

Take a deep breath and, guided by the angelic beings who are with you right now as you begin this journey into the history of your soul, let yourself open up and feel the experience.

***

Before the Beginning

And so it was, beyond time and space, that there was this thing called Spirit. It was Oneness. It was complete unto Itself. Spirit knew nothing other than Itself. It simply existed. It simply was.

Remember here that there is truly no time. Instead, in the realms of the angels and of Spirit, things are marked by experience. So during this journey you can replace your linear timeframe with the timeframe of Spirit, which is experience. Experiences follow one after another after another, and that is how time is known by Spirit.

So at the beginning of all experience, at the beginning of All That Was, there was Oneness. There was Is-ness. There was Completeness.

We use the term "All That Was" because it is no more. No longer can you go back to that original Oneness; it is but a memory. No longer can you return to what we call Home, because Home has changed so much. No longer can you try to get back, because back is now here. Was now Is.

Take a deep breath and feel the energy of All That Was.

Feel the energy of Spirit in completion.

***

This completion went on for what would seem like an eternity in human time, but actually it was in no time at all. Then, in a moment of sheer brilliance, passion and love, this Was-ness asked Itself, "Who am I?"

And what happened then is the history of All That Was and All That Is. When Spirit, Oneness, Love and Completeness asked that single question, "Who Am I?" Its energy burst forth in an incredible brilliance of self-love, self-wonderment, and a desire to express Itself such as it had never known or needed to do.

When Spirit, the original, Eternal One, said, "Who am I?" It instantly created a mirror of Itself so that It could see who It was in order to answer Its own question. And in that mirror the Oneness gazed into Its own heart and instantly fell in love. It fell in love with all that It had been and all that It could ever be. The Oneness fell so deeply in love with Itself that It manifested Its expression.

You see, up until now All That Was had never expressed Itself; It just was.

It never contemplated Itself; It just was.

It never had a desire to know more about Itself; It just was.

But now that the question "Who am I?" had been asked, Oneness created Its own expression, and today we call that the King and the Queen, the Mother-Father God. The Oneness created the incredible ability to see Itself through Another, to experience Itself through the expression of Itself, and now we have the metaphor of Spirit as the King and the Queen.

All That Was has now turned into a Beingness.

You see, by contemplating Itself and falling so deeply in love with Itself, It no longer just was; It began to be. It was an expression.

The King and the Queen fell madly in love with each other, because they were each other. When they gazed into each other's eyes they saw nothing but perfection and beauty, because it was their own perfection and beauty. When they served each other, they were really serving themselves. And when they shared with each other, it was like sharing with themselves. This was the perfect expression, the perfect mirror of love that they had, and they loved each other so dearly.

This passion and love that they had for each other caused something to swell and open up within them, and now they had the desire to share this love. They had found it with each other and enjoyed every moment, every breath, every experience with each other, but now there came the desire to share this. For what is expression, what is creativity and what is love if it cannot be shared with another?

The Children of God

Through this miraculous process of loving each other, which was ultimately loving themselves, they created the children of God. It was the grand birthing of souled beings. You see, even the King and the Queen, the Mother-Father God, aren't souled beings. They are All That Is, but in their tremendous love and their desire to share, they chose to give full expression and full freedom to their children, to all souled beings.

When they birthed these children of God, they gave them no rules and no laws. They didn't tell their children what to do and what not to do. They didn't even tell them that they had to honor the King and the Queen. They gave them one thing: freedom. Freedom to express, freedom to love, freedom to experience, freedom to do whatever they chose, freedom to love Spirit as Spirit loved them, even freedom to turn their back on Spirit if they chose.

Each and every child of God, every souled being was given the essence, the purity, the depth and the light of Spirit. That was Mother-Father God's way of sharing themselves, for they knew that in order to share in the fullest of love, in the fullest of compassion, they couldn't limit their expressions. They didn't need to control their expressions. They didn't need to make these children of God get on their knees and worship them, because the King and the Queen already loved themselves. They had nothing to prove. They had nothing to gain other than the beauty of knowing every one of their expressions would someday realize the same thing that they had realized.

Every souled being, every child of God, sooner or later, in their own way, would one day come to know that they are God also. Every child of God would, at some point, come to know that they have the same creatorship, and that it could never be taken away. Every child of God would come to know the brilliance and the beauty of creation. Every child of God would eventually come to know the same love within that the King and the Queen had for themselves.

Every child of God would someday come to know that they are a full creator. No matter what experiences they had on the way to getting there, no matter how difficult or how dark their path might be, they would someday come to know they are God also. They would come to know the tremendous love and freedom that the King and Queen had.

So it was that we were created – without laws, without rules, without needs – simply from the love and expression of Spirit.

As we go into our story, into this metaphor about your own experience, allow yourself to feel it. It is about the journey that has taken you from Home all the way to Earth. It is about this next doorway that you're going to be crossing through, the doorway of releasing yourself from the clothing and illusion of being just a human and opening yourself up to the fullness of Spirit; knowing that your choices can manifest as easily as you can breathe them into your heart; knowing that there is no judgment for your past; knowing that there is never another challenge that you have to go through unless you choose to.

The Kingdom of I Am

So here you were in the Kingdom of I Am, in the love of Mother-Father Spirit. Here you were in this fantastic realm that the King and Queen had created just for you. It was your playground where you spent each day in the loving arms of Spirit who had no judgment of you other than love, who had no needs or desires other than for you to experience what they had created for you.

Each day you received the love and the tenderness of Spirit. They invited you to go out, to experience and learn about creation, and we call this the First Circle. It was All That Was. It was the Kingdom. It was beautiful beyond words, and they asked you each day to go out and experience and absorb what they had created for you. And you did.

Each day you kissed Mother-Father Spirit goodbye. You told them you would be back at the end of your adventures that day to tell them everything that you had experienced, seen, and felt. Then you would wander off into the beauty and majesty of the First Circle.

Every day you would return back to the light of the Kingdom, to the castle of the King and Queen, and they would receive you with open arms and anticipation, for they wanted to hear what you had experienced. They knew their own Kingdom, but not like you had come to know it. They knew the depth, the width, the dimensionality of the First Circle of the Kingdom, but they had never walked in it themselves. They felt it in their heart, but they had never gone out like you were now going out, experiencing the essence of love in this magical Kingdom.

Every day when you returned and sat down with the King and Queen, you could see the smile on their face. You could feel their fulfillment as you shared the stories of all the things you had seen and felt in the magical experiences of the First Circle.

This went on and on and on, and every day you would explore a new part of creation. Every day you would feel the love and every day you would feel that yearning to go back Home and tell your stories to Spirit. It was magical. It was perfection. It was without any need or want or desire, other than to just be.

You, a souled being, a spirit in your own right, were the beingness part of Spirit. Through you, Spirit could *be* rather than just be an Is. Through you, Spirit could learn and feel and know, rather than just be in the state of Is-ness, and it was beautiful.

The Love of Spirit

And so it was that a new day came. You gave a kiss to the Queen and the King, your spiritual parents. You gave them an extra hug that day because you were so excited about going off and visiting yet a new part of the First Circle of All That Was. You were excited about what these experiences would bring. You had never felt anything like fear, uncertainty or imbalance. It was simply about going out and experiencing, expanding and growing. So on this day you gave them an extra big hug and bid them farewell.

You could feel their love and their tenderness and, as you walked out of the chamber of the King and Queen, you looked back once more to see their smiles, to feel their love and encouragement. But when you looked back at the King and Queen, an unusual thing happened. For the first time ever, you saw a tear in their eye. You felt, for the very first time, something called sadness.

It was an emotion for which you had no frame of reference. It had never been there before and it felt unusual. It felt empty, in a place where you had never felt emptiness. It felt cold, where you had always felt warm and comfortable. It felt disconnected in a way that you didn't know how to describe, but in a way that would haunt you for a long, long time to come.

You took a second glance back at Spirit and this time they were smiling, and you once again felt love. You thought that perhaps, just perhaps, you were mistaken when you saw that tear in their eye, so you continued walking out of the castle, ready to explore, eager about the day had in store, and ready to see new parts of the Kingdom. There was a skip and dance in your step, but something seemed to follow you.

And so it was that you left the Kingdom for the last time.

NOTES

NOTES

CHAPTER 2

LEAVING HOME

And so it was, on this beautiful day, you went out from the castle of the King and the Queen, out from their loving arms. The last thing you saw was the beautiful smile on their face as they bid you farewell, as they gave you the loving wishes from their heart.

The Grandest Adventure

As you walked out for another day of exploration and adventure within the Kingdom, you felt a slight breeze come over your back yet somehow encompassing every part of you. Little did you know that at this very moment the King and Queen, as they were bidding you goodbye, were also breathing life into you.

They were breathing a life into you that would sustain you beyond the edges of the Kingdom. It was a life that would create the awareness of yourself long after you were gone from the Kingdom, that you could always use to breathe life into yourself, no matter where you were or what you were doing, whether it was in your darkest hours or the time of your greatest joy. In this instant, this breath of Spirit became part of you.

As you left the castle, the King and the Queen communicated with each other in a way that you couldn't perceive. They said, "This is the finest day – oh, perhaps sad as well, but this is the finest day – for our dear child goes out to discover who they are. They go out for experience that will change the very nature of the Kingdom and All That Is. No longer will this just be an Is-ness, it will *be*. It will be reality, it will be creation, it will be the expression of all of our love."

As you walked away from the castle and faded from their sight, the King and the Queen gave each other a knowing look and said, "No matter what happens, no matter where your journeys will take you, no matter what things you will choose for your experiences in order to understand who you are, you will get to where you are going. You will become sovereign. You will become a creator of all things. You will create your own heavens. You will create your own grand reality. No matter what occurs along the path of your creations, no matter what kind of experiences – high or low, far or near – that you give yourself, you will get to where you are going. No matter what. It is the way of Spirit. It is the way of love. It is the way of the free and sovereign soul which you will become when you choose."

That day you wandered into parts of the Kingdom that you had never gone into before. It was a grand and glorious day, and you were so captivated by the crystalline energies of the pure consciousness of Spirit that you soon forgot about the tear you thought you had seen earlier. You were captivated by what we might call the colors, but they were far beyond colors, and they were colors that you hadn't seen in any of your other explorations of the kingdom.

Oh, this was long before thought even existed. It was just consciousness, and you were overwhelmed and amazed by the crystalline music of consciousness you heard on this day. You had been out many, many times before, wandering around creation, discovering what Spirit had given and created for you, but today everything was more intense and more real.

You almost felt you could actually touch these things – the crystalline forms of music and color, the crystalline forms of what would later become energies and feelings and awareness and emotion – and you had never had that sensation before. It had always been beautiful, but it wasn't quite as real as what you were experiencing on this day.

So your journey took you to new places, far beyond where you had ever wandered before, and you were making a type of remembrance or note to yourself. You couldn't wait to tell the King and Queen, at the end of your journey today, about the amazing things you saw. You were going to ask them "Why did it seem more real than ever before?

Why did it seem like there was something within me that could touch these things, that could become absorbed in them, that could make them feel so real that it was difficult to find the line between illusion and reality?" You felt within yourself, "I must talk to Spirit about these when I return from this journey."

As you wandered throughout the day, absolutely amazed at everything you were perceiving and absorbing, bringing it into the deepest parts of your soul, little did you know that these were also the seeds of remembrance of the Kingdom. These were the very finest and purest of all the crystalline energies that would become the reminders of Home. And little did you know on that day that this was also preparing you for something that you would encounter much, much later, something called reality, It would be a reality beyond the illusion, beyond being just ethereal, a reality so real that you don't know where to draw the line between yourself and your creations. So all of these seeds of consciousness were being implanted within you to be used later.

A New Frontier

Suddenly your wanderings came to a halt. You had gone farther than you had ever gone before, and now it seemed that everything ended. It would be as if you were wandering through a wonderful forest on a beautiful sunny day, and suddenly came to the end of land, to a beach, and beyond the beach it appeared to be an eternal ocean. That's what it felt like to you right now in the Kingdom. You were on the very edge and it was amazing. You had never felt or seen anything like this before, an endless sea of blue, shimmering, crystalline energy, so overwhelming that you gasped. It was your first deep breath.

There was part of you that felt a deep desire to go out onto this ocean. You wanted to know what that was like, for you had always been in the "land-form" of creation, the consciousness of the Kingdom, and now here was something that appeared to be different and beyond. That desire seemed to pull you out towards the sea. As your natural spiritual curiosity grew, you imagined drifting out onto this beautiful ocean.

Then you heard a voice within you, a voice unlike any you had ever heard before. It felt like it was yours, but it also felt different somehow. It felt like it was coming from the outside, but yet it was so deep within you. It said, "Do not go. Do not venture out, for you are safe here in the Kingdom. You know the Kingdom, you are safe with the King and Queen, and each night you can rest in their arms. If you go out onto this ocean, we cannot tell you what will happen."

You paused, but yet the appeal of going out where you had never ventured before, out into these beautiful crystalline waters, was so overwhelming that it pulled at every part of you. And, as you were trying to decide whether to stay or to go, suddenly a little boat appeared out of nowhere. It just came drifting over towards you, beckoning you. There was something inside you that felt, "If the boat appeared, then it must be right. It must be a sign that I should go out and venture onto this ocean." And in your excitement and enthusiasm for going out onto this sea of consciousness, you forgot that other voice.

Well, as you sit here now, you are very familiar with that voice. You hear that voice almost every time you come to a Point of Separation or a point of choice in your life. You hear that voice every time you leave the familiar comfort of your current moment to venture into something new. You think sometimes the voice is Spirit, or a demon, or the part of you that's protecting you. Or you think perhaps it is just good common sense. But the voice you heard that first time, standing on the very edge of the ocean of new consciousness, is still with you.

As the boat drifted toward you, magically drifting right up onto the shore in front of you, you forgot about the voice. And, as you crawled into the boat, you felt such a sense of freedom, such a sense of discovery that your own heart and its desires now started leading you out onto the sea.

Sailing

It was a beautiful day. The ocean was calm. There was hardly a wave on the water, just enough gentle rocking motion of the ocean to soothe your being, to gently rock you and give you a little reminder of Spirit rocking you, holding you, comforting you. And the desire in your soul caused the boat to go a little bit further and then a little bit further from land.

As the excitement and tension were building, you were giving yourself all these reminders about what you were going to tell Spirit when you returned back Home. You would tell the King and Queen about the excitement of getting into the boat, how the boat magically appeared and how now it was going out on its own. All you had to do was desire and the boat would go. All you had to do was desire to be out further and further into the sea of consciousness, and the boat went. It was amazing. It was the first time you remembered actually creating something for yourself, because all this time, back in the Kingdom, you had simply been viewing and exploring what Spirit had created for you. But now, you felt your own creation as the boat was moving.

It was a beautiful day. There was just enough gentle breeze to refresh your inner being, just enough motion on the waves to give you comfort, just the right amount of light so that you could feel and perceive everything around you. It was the most glorious moment you could ever recall. You felt the excitement, the laughter, the happiness, the joy and the freedom of being on this sea of consciousness.

You wondered if Spirit even knew about this place. The King and Queen had never mentioned it to you before, maybe even they didn't know about this sea of consciousness. It was the finest, finest moment, and you settled down into the bottom of the boat just to take it all in, just to be filled with all of these sensations and awarenesses and love and excitement of this glorious adventure that you were having. You only wished right now that you could just share it with somebody, but you were sure there would be plenty of opportunities to do that later.

A Dream

As the boat drifted further and further out onto the ocean of consciousness, you lost sight of the land. It was so far in the distance on the horizon that it didn't even show up anymore, but that didn't concern you. And as you drifted further and further out onto the ocean, you became sleepy.

Even before you got into this little boat, it had already been a long day of exploring the crystalline energies of the Kingdom, and now you were sleepy. You were growing tired, but in such a beautiful, happy way. You let your spiritual eyes close. You let yourself totally relax and you started to do your breathing, something you had just discovered. What a joy to breathe, to feel consciousness flow into you. And as you started breathing, you became sleepier.

As you were breathing, with the boat gently rocking, you became even sleepier.

And as the beautiful light that surrounded everything seemed to radiate directly on you, you got even sleepier.

You could hear beautiful music playing all around, a sort of humming or resonance that you had never heard before, coming from the ocean itself, and it caused you to get sleepier and sleepier.

As you were laying there in the bottom of the boat on this grand day, you surrendered yourself to sleep, gently going further and further out onto the ocean.

As you went into this deep sleep, something occured that had never happened to you before. You would understand it now as a dream, but you had never dreamed before back in the Kingdom. There was no need to dream, it simply was that it was. Everything was complete unto itself. But now, as you fell into this deep sleep in the boat, you had a dream of soaring, of flying.

In your dream you had wings. You were majestic and free, soaring through the skies. All you had to do was feel where you wanted to go and you would be there. Your wings could take you anywhere.

You were laying in the bottom of the boat having this dream, experiencing something you had never known back in the Kingdom, experiencing being a majestic white and gold bird with huge wings, just floating. There was no effort. You simply floated anywhere you wanted to go, guided by something deep within you that created a reality any time you felt or thought about something.

It was a beautiful dream, even though you wondered what this experience was. Were you back in the Kingdom? Was this experience coming from inside you or was it something the King and Queen were giving to you? Even though you didn't know the answer, you allowed the experience to continue because it was so magnificent.

Then suddenly everything shifted. You tried to pull out of it, but the dream became stronger than anything else you could desire or feel. And then, everything in the dream suddenly went dark. This golden soaring bird that was you suddenly seemed to shrink in size and turn black.

As you struggled against the darkness, your beautiful golden wings began to shrink. They become very brittle, very fragile, until suddenly they were ripped away from you. The next thing you remember was endless falling. You were being pulled into something against your will, against your desire, when suddenly you woke up in the boat, wondering what had just happened.

What was that experience that you just had? It felt like an illusion, but yet it felt so very real. It felt like you were really experiencing it, but yet how could you be? You were here in the boat, out on the ocean of consciousness in this beautiful place called the Kingdom, and all seemed well. So you shrugged it off and made a note to ask Spirit about this when you returned back Home later in the day. For now, you would just let yourself experience this beautiful ocean.

The Storm

You sat up in the boat, looked out, and were surprised to see dark clouds up ahead, and you were going toward them. "Well," you thought to yourself, "it's time to turn back. I've gone as far as I should go. I've had some very unusual and amazing experiences today, but now I desire to go back Home."

You put it out again – "I desire to go back Home."

Yet a third time you took a deep breath and said, "I desire to go back Home. I desire now to be back with the King and Queen, for this day has been very long." But the boat did not turn around. Instead you felt it speeding up.

As you were looking out on the horizon, you saw very dark, angry clouds coming in. The sea was not as calm as it was when you first got into the boat, and now it was starting to develop waves and commotion. Instead of being peaceful and calm, it was choppy and you didn't like the experience at all. It was putting you off balance, and this was not at all what you wanted to create.

Maybe it was just an experience. Maybe it was just some element of the Kingdom, but you didn't like it and it was time to turn around. Yet still the boat kept going further and further, and the storm clouds kept drawing closer and closer. Now you began to see something like lightning within the clouds. You could see this intense type of orange-red color leaping through them, and this did not feel good at all.

You had never before experienced an ill or negative feeling, or anything like the fear that was now starting to come in. But, deep within, you still felt that you would be safe, that it was just another experience in the Kingdom. So you took a deep breath and commanded the boat to turn around and go back to shore.

You commanded with all of your might from the deepest parts of you, yet the boat just started going faster, further away from the Kingdom, closer to these approaching storm clouds. And as you got closer, they appeared even angrier. They weren't just dark and ominous black clouds. There was something like flames coming from deep within them, like fire rising from the ocean itself into these storm clouds, and it didn't feel good at all.

You took another deep breath and this time you called out to Spirit as you had never done before. "Dear Spirit, hear me now, Mother-Father God, for I am in a place where I don't want to be. Dear Spirit, Mother-Father God, this is your Kingdom. Bring me back. Bring me away from whatever dangers lie ahead, for I have no experience with danger. I have no experience with dealing with these things, and it appears beyond me, a child of God, so I leave it in your hands."

You sat down in the bottom of the boat for a moment, waiting to be pulled back Home, but nothing happened.

You didn't feel any sense of the presence of Spirit. The boat didn't turn around. You didn't hear the loving voice of the King and the Queen.

Can't Go Back

Now, sitting in the bottom of the boat, you felt something else come over you, a feeling that you didn't like at all, for it felt dark and empty and cruel. You felt guilt and shame.

You knew at this moment that you should have listened to that voice deep within, for it had told you not to venture out onto the ocean of consciousness. You knew it must have been the voice of Spirit, but you had gone against it, and now look what was happening.

As this guilt and shame came over you, you promised to never, ever turn your back on Spirit again, to never go against the word of Spirit, to never ignore that deep inner voice ever again. You promised over and over andover to never again disobey Spirit.

And now, sitting in the bottom of the boat, you did something for the first time that you've done many, many times since. You prayed.

Calling out to Spirit, you begged, "Dear Spirit, hear me, feel me. Spirit, I am sorry for what I have done. I beg your forgiveness. Spirit, I know I have done wrong. I know I have been bad. Bring me back into your loving arms and I will do nothing but honor and worship and love you and do whatever you ask. But dear Spirit, something is happening right now. Bring me back home, please."

Nothing happened, other than the storm seemed to get closer. The waves now were becoming violent, and what had been beautiful music on this sea of consciousness was now angry thunder and rumbling, and it was getting closer and closer.

"Where is Spirit?" you cried. "I have called out to Father-Mother God. I have prayed on my hands and knees. I have made a solemn oath to never, ever do this again. I will never even leave the castle. I will never venture into the Kingdom again. Dearest Spirit, hear me now. Hear me now, Spirit. If you love me, if you remember me, hear me now. This is when I need you."

You crawled up from the bottom of the boat and looked back toward where you had come from, back toward land, but there was nothing. It too had gone dark. You looked ahead to where the boat was heading and saw a wall of fire rising from the ocean. It was surrounded by the storm clouds and you knew that nothing within you now could turn you around. It was only the love of Spirit that could save you. You knew that this was your final moment.

You came closer and closer, and as you were about ready to collide into this wall of fire, into this terror, into this darkness and rage, you screamed out one final time from every part of you. "Now, Spirit! Now!"

And so it was.

NOTES

NOTES

Chapter 3

The Wall of Fire

And so it was, in that moment before you collided with the Wall of Fire, above the noise and the thunder of this tremendous force that lay before you, above even the fear within you, that you did indeed hear an answer. You heard a voice from Home that said, "You will never be alone."

Then you were drawn into the Wall of Fire with such a ferocious force that it tore you apart. It had strength. You were bewildered that it could shred you – not just toss you and turn you, but tear you apart – and at the deepest levels of your soul, you felt yourself ripped into a hundred pieces. And each of those pieces were ripped into a thousand pieces, and every one of those pieces ripped into a million and then a billion pieces.

And when, in the midst of all of this chaos, you thought to take a breath, the wave of shredding and shattering came over you again and tore you once again into billions and billions of other pieces. There seemed no hope. There seemed no way to get out, and every time you tried to regain your balance and call out to Home, you were torn apart again and again, over and over.

In what seemed like an endless amount of time, these energies of the Wall of Fire continued to tear you and shred you. Every time you tried to regain your essence and your identity, it would tear you apart once again. You had never felt anything like this. You had never known a force so brutal and so destructive on the very core of your soul.

Waves and waves and waves of these vicious energies kept coming over you. Every time you tried to come up for a breath, it would pull you under again. Every time you tried to collect some of the pieces that were being ripped away, even more would be ripped from you again.

The Shadow

During the midst of all of this commotion and pain and terror, you saw something out of the corner of your soul eye that you had never seen before. For the briefest moment you saw something that you now know as your shadow. You connected instantly with that shadow, and you knew in that moment exactly what it was. It was your shame and your guilt. It was your fear. It was the deepest nightmares you thought you could ever possibly have, but you had never experienced anything like it.

The moment you saw that shadow of yourself, you tried to run and hide from it, because you felt deep within you that it was this shadow, this darkness that was causing all of the terror in the Wall of Fire. But the moment you tried to run from it, it came closer, even though everything else was being torn into pieces in this storm that never ended. It was like a hurricane and a tornado combined together, ripping you over and over, tearing you into smaller and smaller pieces.

Infinite Potentials

In this experience in the Wall of Fire, which seemed eternal, never-ending and hopeless, you experienced and felt every potential of every lifetime you were ever going to live, every angelic family you would ever know, every thought you would ever think, and every desire that would ever occur to you. As you were being torn into these billions and billions of pieces, every piece represented a potential of every feeling you would ever have, every decision you might ever make. In these potentials were all of the paths that you would ever take, and all of the paths that you would never take.

The shattering and tearing continued as every potential was shattered into more pieces, more potentials within potentials, and the entire time you were trying to scream out. But nothing – no sound, no feeling, nothing – came out. You felt like you were trying to run and hide, but every time this Wall of Fire would find you and drag you back into its core and tear you into more pieces.

The shattering continued for what seemed forever.

It was shredding all hope. It was shredding every experience you had ever had back at Home. It was tearing apart your memories of the King and Queen. It was demolishing and destroying everything that you had felt or seen or come to know back in the Kingdom, mutilating them beyond all recognition.

Every time you gasped out for breath, trying to bring life back into yourself, another wave of shattering came over you. At last you came to the point where, in this eternal nightmare, this eternal shattering of Self, you gave up.

Letting Go
You let go. You weren't trying to keep ahead of it anymore, because every time you did it would drag you under and rip you apart again. You stopped trying to remember your times at Home, because every time you did it was too painful. You stopped trying to connect with any of the potentials, because they seemed so foreign and so distant. Even though they seemed familiar, you didn't want to go into any of these potentials. You didn't want to try to hide in them, because you were afraid that they would turn into a reality.

Every time you tried to pull away from all this chaos, it would pull you back in with tremendous force and then smash you into ever more pieces.

So, you let go of hope. You let go of desire. You let go of trying to maintain any sense of Self or Home. You knew this was the end.

You gave one last grand effort to find or wish or desire your way back out, back to the arms of the King and Queen. It was one last gallant effort to bring yourself back Home. But, when you found yourself drawing some type of inner strength to find that memory and connect into it, this Wall of Fire grabbed every part of you, strangling and suffocating and smashing you into even more pieces.

At that point you let go. You surrendered.

There wasn't another ounce of strength within you. There wasn't another feeling of desire. There wasn't any more recollection of yourself or anything you had ever been. Now you just allowed yourself to fall into the darkness, into the nothingness. You allowed yourself now to plunge into what felt like the death of Self, the destruction of anything and everything that you had ever known or felt.

You let go. And, as you let go, the storm slowly began to subside and go away.

Now you found yourself in nothing.

Darkness.

Cold.

Absolutely alone.

Nothing.

This was a nightmare even worse than the Wall of Fire itself, because now it was empty. Nothing was left. Any part of an identity of yourself was completely gone.

So empty, it wasn't even dark anymore. It was nothing.

You were fading away.

Dying.

Nothing left.

You were gone.

No longer did you exist.

And so it was.

NOTES

NOTES

CHAPTER 4

AWAKENING

And so it was that the storms in the Wall of Fire subsided and you entered into nothingness. What you felt was the loss of your own existence. It was beyond darkness; there was absolutely nothing at all.

If you look deep into your soul self right now in this moment, you will realize that this was the most difficult moment that you have ever been through. This experience of absolute nothingness is the deepest wound and the largest fear that any angel or any human will ever know.

Part of you actually wanted to be back in the Wall of Fire, even with all of its chaos and agony and shattering. In spite of the fact that the Wall of Fire was a tremendous storm that ripped you into pieces, tore you apart and denied you of getting yourself back together, at least in the Wall of Fire you felt the essence of your existence. You knew you were still a being, that you were still living in some form. Although it was terrible, awful and violent, at least you existed. But now, as the storm subsided, you felt yourself falling into darkness, into the abyss, falling out of existence itself.

There was not anything external to you that created any sort of activity or impulse. There was nothing anywhere around you. You couldn't even feel yourself. It was utterly dark, empty, cold. All feeling of life force energy had been pulled out. You were absolutely alone. There was nothing, anywhere.

Even right now as a human on Earth, this is still the deepest wound from your darkest moment. You still run from the fear that this may happen again. This memory of going out of existence is why humans fear death. They do not understand what happens beyond physical death and therefore fear that they will go back into this coldest, emptiest abyss that they've ever felt. It is truly the largest wound.

So many humans fill their life with drama and emotion and external activity because they feel if they stop for even a moment, they're going to go back into the darkness. There is something deep within every being that fears getting sucked back into the Void.

Nothing

So here you are in absolute nothingness. You can feel a part of you trying to rebuild the recollection of Home, to retrieve the memory of the King and Queen, but when you do, it simply goes to nothing. When you try to recall your voyage in the little boat out on the sea of consciousness, it goes blank. There is nothing. When you try to go back into the Wall of Fire, trying to retrace your footsteps back to this vague, faint memory of Home, it goes to nothing.

There is only darkness.

You are totally alone.

Even when you try to breathe life into yourself, it seems to be sucked right back out by this Void you are in.

In a sense, it isn't even terrifying, because even terror has no place here in this abyss. Even when you try to bring up a sense of fear, it is pulled out and goes back into nothingness. The nothingness seems to suck everything right out of you. As much as you try to be alive and make yourself exist, it goes back into absolute nothingness.

Even now, in the moment you are reading this, you still feel that pull of nothingness deep within. You still feel that sense of going out of existence.

This time that you spent in nothingness was timeless, because even time, with a sense of the sequence of experience, was pulled out, was absolutely nothing.

Why is it that children and even adults are so often afraid of the dark? Why is it that so many humans are restless at night when they sleep? It is because they still fear and are running from this nothingness. Even in their sleep at night they can't settle down. They have to keep the wheels turning, no matter what kind of dreams or activities they might have, because the fear of going back into nothingness is still so great.

It is because of this fear that humans and angels alike build activities all around them to distract themselves and to keep reminding themselves that they are alive.

The Shadow

Dear one, you no longer have to fear going back into nothingness or going out of existence, because, as you were absolutely alone in the Void, something occurred. You suddenly felt a presence. You didn't have physical eyes back then, but you noticed something. It was a shadow, the same shadow that you had seen for just an instant back in the Wall of Fire, and here it was, with you again.

The shadow caused you to feel something within, and just having that feeling renewed you, and you realized maybe you weren't completely out of existence.

It was a moment unlike any other because it was such a contrast to the emptiness and the abyss around you. And in that beautiful, sacred moment, you suddenly realized "I Am! Although there is a Void and darkness all around me, I can hear my thoughts and I just saw the shadow of myself."

In this beautiful moment you realized, "If I can hear my own thoughts and feel myself, therefore I *do* exist. I don't know where I exist, I don't know what I am in, I don't know where I came from, I don't even know who I am, but I must exist. I can feel myself. I am aware of me. There's nothing else around, but suddenly I am aware. I don't know how to get out of this, but I Am. I am here, right now; therefore, I exist. Therefore, I Am."

In this beautiful moment of transformation, created by the simplest thought a human or angel will ever have – "I Am" – the life force burst up from a place within you that you hadn't even known existed. The energy of Spirit, the consciousness of the I Am, suddenly rose up and you felt Self. You felt existence at the simplest and purest level that you would not feel again for a long, long time to come. You felt that life-force energy rush within you and now, when you took a breath, you felt yourself. You didn't know who you were or why you were, but you knew that you were, and in this moment you had hope.

In this moment you felt a freedom, a liberation that was difficult to define. You felt a sudden desire to experience something, anything, to express, to call out from your soul and say, "I have awoken. I am here." Even if nothing or no one could hear you or feel you, at least your soul could rejoice, "I Am! I Exist!" And, in contrast to the moment before where there was nothingness, now you had one of the most beautiful and joyful experiences of consciousness that you will ever have.

However, there is still this shadow of yourself, the shadow that you took from Home, that came with you through the Wall of Fire, that you felt in the abyss. Even now this shadow sometimes overshadows the potential for joy in your life, the potential to say, "I Am! I Exist, therefore I Am, and that's all that's needed." There is still a fear in both humans and angels that if you rejoice in the I Am-ness of your existence, it may be pulled back into the abyss, into the darkness and the nothingness.

So humans and angels alike are fearful of proclaiming "I Am that I Am" because they feel that perhaps it will pull them into the nothingness. But it won't. When you proclaim "I Am that I Am," when you declare your existence, it brings up consciousness, the gift that Spirit gave you as a souled, sovereign being.

The Sovereign Self

When you first realized your own existence in the Void, you had a sense of freedom, of wanting to express, wanting to know who you were. And this desire helped solidify your soul.

Contained within your soul is the essence of Spirit, but it belongs only to you.

Within your soul is the love of Spirit, but now it is all the potential of loving yourself and who you are, just as Spirit loved Itself.

Within your soul is all of the potential to create anything you choose for yourself, just as Spirit could create for Itself anything It chose.

Within yourself is the ability to ask, "Who am I?" and then take a journey that lasted eons of time (but actually no time at all) in the discovery of who you are.

Within the soul Self is the ability to see yourself, to create the mirror of yourself, just as Spirit created the mirror of Itself, so that you can see your own expression. This way you can experience yourself, including every thought, every choice, and every path. This is all contained within the soul – your soul – that now was birthed.

Within the soul is its sovereign beingness, which means that you are complete unto yourself. There is no need to bring in consciousness from another or bring in energy from outside of you.

Within the sovereign divine soul, everything is complete.

Within the sovereign, divine self, the soul of you, is the ability to love yourself so deeply by creating mirror images of yourself; by creating a feminine aspect and a masculine aspect who will eventually love each other so deeply that you'll realize the intense and pure and real love that Spirit has for Spirit.

All of these things are yours.

Within this sovereign self, within your complete divine being, is the absolute ability to transform into anything you want and to rejuvenate any imbalances. This ability is contained within each and every one of us, because it is also the essence of Spirit.

Contained within your sovereign being is the ability to always be free, to always be your own oneness, to always be a creator. And also contained within your sovereign being is the consciousness that no one can ever take this away from you. Ever. They have tried and you have allowed them to try. You have gone through many experiences to see if it was possible for another being to take away your consciousness and your soul – oh, the games have been played of stealing energy and consciousness – but in the end, nobody can.

Contained within your sovereignty is absolute resolution. You can never stray off the path. You can create the illusion that you are straying off the path, but you can never go wrong. You can try to go wrong, you can pretend to go wrong, but ultimately you cannot. In the I Am essence, the consciousness of "I Am That I Am," the journey is already complete.

You've already achieved your sovereignty in this moment right now. In the Void where you first realized the I Am-ness of your existence, you already completed your journey. But now, this loving, beautiful pure part of yourself has the desire to express and experience, for that's what Spirit does. Spirit, in love with Itself, continually expresses and continually experiences, and that is where you're at right now.

Beyond All That Was

You're outside the Wall of Fire. You have left All That Was and gone beyond the consciousness of Spirit itself. You left the First Circle, where even Spirit has never ventured. It is the Void, and it is the gift and the love of Spirit. You're no longer in the Kingdom. In fact you could say that nothing exists here, because Spirit has never been here. You have chosen to go beyond All That Was in order to understand your own sovereignty, in order to create your own path, and also, out of love to Spirit Itself, to share your experiences.

Now, you've gone outside of all creation, outside of consciousness, outside of All That Was. It could be said that even Spirit doesn't know where you are. Spirit only knows that you are. And in this moment, outside of All That Was, you're about to embark on a beautiful expression of your soul.

Here, outside of all consciousness, you will never go Home again. Part of you knew this, and felt both the excitement and the sadness of knowing that you will never again go Home.

It is true that over eons of time, lifetimes in physical reality and lifetimes in the angelic realms, you will constantly share and communicate your experiences back to Spirit. But, while there is a constant link to Spirit, you will never go back Home. And at this moment, outside the Wall of Fire, outside the First Circle, something inside you knows that, and this causes a great sadness.

As much as there is a desire to express yourself, there is also now a desire to get back Home. But, just like your experience back at the edge of land before you set off in the little boat out on the sea of consciousness, the part of you that wants to experience your I Am-ness and to know yourself is so strong, so overwhelming, that you burst forth with life. There is no going Home because that would be a dishonor to the very reason Spirit gave you life and freedom. Instead of going Home, one day Home will come to you.

At this moment, in what you might now describe as color, music, feeling – an absolute awareness in a very pure state – it was as if you birthed yourself. This moment of expansion created both an inner looking Self and your outer expression.

The Inner Self and the Outer Expression

You now understand the inner looking Self as your divinity, and this pure absolute essence of your Self was put into a type of cocoon in order to take an inner look. It would explore the inner realms, the essence, the soul, the divine, the consciousness of you, while the outer expression would now go forth into the Void. It didn't know how or why or what would happen, but its desire for expression was so overwhelming that it burst forth. This outer expression of you would eventually create every experience that you would ever have.

In this moment of absolute awareness of Self, you opened up. You blossomed. You started expanding, while at the same time the inner looking Self went inside to understand your consciousness, your divine, your relationship to Spirit, your essence as Spirit.

The inner looking Self would constantly feel every experience you would ever create, totally without judgment or analysis. It would simply be aware. And the inner looking Self would also constantly flow this new consciousness of you back to Spirit so that someday Home could come to you. Yes, you would never return back Home, but someday Home would come back to you.

So here you were in the absolute Void, free, newly birthed, wanting to express your I Am-ness, breathing once again but this time outside of All That Was. You were here with the shadow self that accompanied you from Home through the Wall of Fire, and now you set out on a journey that would last eons of time.

You took a deep breath, deep within your soul, and said, "I Am aware of myself." And then you said the words that launched you forth on your journey: "Who am I?"

And so it was.

NOTES

NOTES

CHAPTER 5

STAR WARS

And so it was, dear angel and dear human, that the Void was actually your playground of potential. It is the gift from Spirit to you, for how could you ever come to know yourself if you had stayed within the Kingdom, the First Circle? This nothingness was a gift of love that Spirit had given you.

Yes, it was terrifying leaving Home. It was terrifying to be aware of all the experiences that you could ever have. It was terrifying to know that you would never go back Home, and a big part of you wanted to stay there. But another part of you, your soul, had the desire to experience and discover yourself. And your soul had such compassion and love for Spirit, for the King and the Queen, that it wanted to go experience on their behalf.

For the Love of Spirit

You see, Spirit couldn't have done this on Its own, not like Spirit could do in and through you, through your compassion and your love. When you were back in the Kingdom you said to Spirit, "I will go forth as a child of God to learn what lies beyond, to learn what it's like to discover Self, to know who I am. And in doing so, dear Spirit, you will also come to know who you are."

So you see, there was no wrong in all of this. There were no bad choices. There was no outside force compelling you to do this. It was the love of Spirit for you that gave you the freedom to go into All That Wasn't, and it was your love for Spirit that said, "I will go and discover who I am, and in doing so, you can discover who you are also."

This was grand perfection. This was love and sharing and compassion in its simplest and purest form. There was no guilt for setting out on the ocean of consciousness and going through the Wall of Fire. There was no shame. There was no judgment from Spirit, for this was an adventure that you and Spirit chose.

So here you are now in the Void, having felt yourself for the first time, having taken your first breath on your own outside of the Kingdom. Here you are, feeling the grand desire to express and rejoice in yourself, and at the same time feeling a deep longing for something. You weren't even sure what it was, but you were feeling the longing for Home, and that longing has been with you ever since.

You had the feeling of separation, like you had been cut off from something, as if you were abandoned or forgotten. But, indeed, you never were. This has always been a journey of choice.

The Boat of Choice

When the boat came to the shore to take you away onto the ocean, it was by your choice and your creation. And even while you called out for the boat to return back to land, there was a deeper, more loving part of you that knew it was appropriate to continue on the journey. The boat is now a symbol of your journey, a symbol of the grandest choice that you have ever made.

Sometimes, in your experience as a human, you wonder why you express a choice and then it doesn't happen. You wonder why certain things don't happen according to the expectation that you might have in the human mind. It is because of a deeper choice of your soul. This choice is symbolized by the original boat that has carried you on this journey and that is going to carry you into your own sovereignty, into the knowingness that you are your own One, and into your full creator ability.

This symbolic boat has always been with you. It has always carried you on the journey and even when the human cries out in prayer with expectations that are limited to the human self, this boat still carries you. It is not Spirit telling you to take this boat; it is yours. You created it, and it is there for your journey.

Indeed, there are times when you step out of that boat and go off wandering, whether as a human or as an angel. But the boat is always there, waiting to carry you. It is your sacred vessel, your true safe space, and it will always be there.

No Mistakes

I'm going to digress for a moment here to share something with you at a very deep level. There are times when you wonder about making mistakes or felt that you have made wrong choices. In fact, you often don't make choices anymore because you're afraid of making the wrong one. But I tell you that you cannot.

Oh yes, you can have many, many experiences, and some of them can be very challenging. We have seen angels that have experienced the darkest of the dark, or a lot of nothingness in their life. We have seen humans and angels alike who've experienced a lot of drama and trauma. This is part of your journey and part of what you are choosing. But ultimately, you always get back into that boat, back into your sacred vessel that takes you closer and closer to your sovereignty. And it is known already by your soul that you will arrive.

You may choose to take many lifetimes with a lot of deviations and different paths to get there, but you will get there. In truth, it is known that you are already there; now you are just going through the experience, for your soul and for Spirit, of what it was like to get there.

That is also why I say that it doesn't matter. All of these things that you take into your life, the things you worry about, the things you fret about – from the big things like death to the little things like the annoyances of your family members and friends – they don't really matter, because you are going to get there anyway.

You are already there. Now, how do you choose to experience it?

All of the little things that you worry about, they are ultimately just adding to your experience. But it doesn't matter. You can get there any way you choose.

Take a deep breath with that, and perhaps it is a wonderful time to let go of your worry.

There's still an angel part of you from a long, long time ago that worries, "Will I ever make it? Will I ever find the completion? Will I ever do as I told Father-Mother God I would do – discover myself?"

From the Order of the Ascended Masters who are there, the answer is "Absolutely. Now, how do you want to get there?"

Divinity

So, here you are in the Void, in absolute nothingness but aware of yourself, aware of your soul. Part of you now has gone within, into a type of cocoon, for a deep inner look. Sometimes this is referred to as the divine or the God within that went to look at the consciousness of everything that you were ever going to experience, looking not at the facts and the figures, but the feelings, consciousness, awareness and evolution of your soul.

This inward-looking part is the library, the feelings and the life of your soul, and the cocoon is a wrapping that keeps it safe. Just as you would put money or valuables in a bank, a safe, or some place to hold them while you went out on a long journey, so you put your divinity into this cocoon so that you could go out and experience. This was so that it could never be damaged or broken, twisted or distorted by any of the experiences that you would choose. It would never be taken over by any of the aspects that you were about to create, and so it would always remain pure.

Now you took another deep breath and began your expressions. It was the true beginning of your journey of coming to know, "Who am I?"

These are amazing words. Remember, there was only oneness, only consciousness, until Spirit said, "Who am I?" Then it burst forth into expression and experience. You, a child of God, now said these very words – "Who am I?" – and the fun began.

Discovering Others

Just as you were feeling yourself and expanding, suddenly you felt another energy, something outside of you. It was a very lovely and beautiful experience, because this other energy now began to give shape to the Void. It wasn't just you and nothingness; you felt something else.

The very awareness of this other essence attracted you to it immediately and suddenly you stood face to face, metaphorically speaking, with another angel. You discovered that there was something else out here with you – a playmate, a friend, another being – and this surprised and delighted you, for then you knew you were not alone.

Well, your energy jumped all over theirs and theirs over you, because you were so delighted to find each other out here in the Void. And right away something within you said, "There's another soul here. I bet *they* know the way Home."

So, after your initial dance or meld with them, you communicated to them, asking, "How do you get Home?" And this other angelic being, much like a little angelic child, said, "I do not know. I'm not even sure that there is a Home, but I've been asking myself the same thing. I've been saying, 'Who am I? And how do I get back Home?' Maybe together we can find out. If we put our energies together, maybe we could find out how to get back Home."

You thought this was a wonderful plan, so you agreed, and then you both just sat there for a while. But nothing happened. Then a thought came over you. "I bet this other angel knows the way back Home, they're just not telling me. Maybe they want to get back Home, but there's not room for both of us. They want Home all to themselves. So maybe I ought to pounce on this being. Maybe I ought to devour their energy and gobble it up and thereby find the answer to help me get back Home."

So, as you were both just kind of sitting there waiting for something to happen, you leapt over, grabbed their consciousness and devoured it. Of course, you didn't have physical bodies, so we speak in metaphor, but you did indeed try to devour that other angelic being. Then a funny thing happened. You noticed that it felt really good! There was a lot of energy there and it made you swell. It made you feel different. It made you feel less alone. It made you feel full, and you really liked the feeling.

We're going to call this feeling 'power.' Now, power is an absolute illusion and always has been, but you felt this power and you liked it. You digested it and let it sit within you for a little while. Then suddenly you felt a kind of torment within you because this other angel didn't like being there, and it started fighting its way out. The more it fought its way out, the more you fought against it, like two little children engaged in a battle. Tumbling and tossing and turning and fighting, each trying to get something from the other, because just as much as you were trying to take energy from this other angel, they were also trying to take it from you.

This went on for a long, long time, until finally you both lay exhausted, neither one able to overcome the other. You see, each one had the same quotient of consciousness or Spirit within you, so how could one overtake the other?

So, you made an agreement with each other. You said, "Let's stop all this fighting and energy stealing and let's begin our search together, because maybe together we can find our way Home better than alone."

Well, before long, you felt another energy come in. Another angel showed up, and you repeated the same process you had done before. It was a delight to feel the presence of another angel, but soon you had the same thought – "They must know the way home" – and you and your friend now tried to devour and steal consciousness from this third little angel. There was tumbling and tossing and turning and trying to steal energy, and it felt wonderful. You even turned on your original friend, even though you had an agreement not to fight anymore, but again it was the same result: nothing happened. You all laid there tired, drained and having gotten nowhere.

Of course, you can already feel the rest of the story, because you know this happened time and time again. Your little group of angels would band together, run into other little angels and repeat the cycle, trying to steal their consciousness and energy. It felt so good it was almost addictive, this trying to devour another being.

In the end it didn't work, because you can't take over another souled being. You can't trap them. You can't eat them and digest them. But, oddly enough, it feels good while you're trying to do it.

Forever Friends

Now, I want to stop here and make a footnote. In the original group of angels that you met, the first few dozen or so, you developed a very strong bond with each other, like no other bond you've known since, because these were the first that you met, the first that you felt outside of Home. And in this process of devouring and trying to digest another angel, you really felt their energy, their uniqueness, and it made you realize something about your own. Even with all the fighting going on, it was actually a beautiful thing because, in the end, there can be no true harm to a souled being. And, through every experience that you had with every other little angel, you learned something about yourself.

This original group of angels that you encountered have been close to you ever since. You've had more lifetimes with them here on Earth than with any other beings. Sometimes they are what you call your spirit guides, because when they are not here on Earth at the same time as you are, you still feel their loving presence. You still feel that original experience and connection that you had with them.

It's interesting to note that, although these angels are like true soul mates to you, meaning that you've shared a lot of lifetimes and experiences together, most often you do not end up marrying these people or even being in the same biological families. The association and connection with them is so deep that you don't choose to have the biological or karmic connection, and they end up being good friends or ones that you may meet and know for just a very short time in your life, but yet you feel so very connected.

These are the beings that you can sometimes feel around you, even if you don't know who they are or haven't spent much time with them. These are the beings you meet who make such an impact on you that you never forget them, even if you didn't spend a lot of time together.

You could say they are your original soul group – not your spiritual family, which is a little different – but your original soul group, and that deep connection is still there.

The Others
So here you are now, with all these little angels. You were like little lost children in a very big, very open and sometimes very dark playground. It was like a little group of angels lost in the woods, all trying to figure your way out, all wanting to get back Home even though you barely remembered Home, but in the meantime playing, fighting, and tumbling together.

This went on and on. Your little group would encounter another little group of angels, and everyone repeated the process. You tried to take over their group and they tried to take over yours. You tried to steal their energy and they tried to steal yours. It went on and on, each time with the same result – nothing. You can't take over a souled being. Yes, you can create the illusion for a little while, but ultimately you cannot enslave, own or possess another souled being.

Now, all this time you were out in the Void, there was nothing out there other than souled beings. And, to answer a question right now, there were a finite number of souled beings who went through the Wall of Fire. It was a large number, but it was finite. There was also a finite amount of what you now call energy that went through the Wall of Fire into the Void. And this finite group of souled beings or angels has been playing with this finite amount of energy ever since – changing it, transmuting it from one form to another – but always with the same quantity of energy and souled beings.

Now, you may ask, "How many souled beings are there outside of Home?" I'll give you a simple answer: One. You are the only one that matters. There might be billions and billions of angels, but it doesn't matter because, in the eyes of Spirit, there is only you. In the evolution of your soul there is only you. Once you start taking responsibility for all of these other souls, it distracts from you. So, remember, how many souled beings are there outside of Home? Just you.

Beginning Creation

So here you are in the Void. It was nothing when you began, but now it was starting to turn into something because of the expressions of you and all the other souled beings. You created dimensions with every thought, every experience and every expression that you had, and these began as non-physical dimensions. They eventually turned into physical dimensions, what you now call your physical universe, but initially these were just dimensions of feeling, thought-forms and experience, and they were being created by you and the other angelic beings.

Soon there came to be something that you now call light. We're not talking about light from the sun or from a light bulb. The light was consciousness, and it was giving grand definition to the realms of the Void. This was the very reason you left Home – to go experience your own creations – and now it was happening.

It was happening at tremendous "speed," although in these realms there was no such thing as speed. It was happening in a way that you would now perceive as incredibly fast, because as fast as you could express, it would happen. As fast as you would have a type of spiritual thought, it would be so.

Now, you can imagine, with these groups and bands of little angels playing and interacting, how fast everything was moving, so much so that it defied any sort of true depth or awareness. Then one day, with all of this commotion and activity going on between all the little angels, something began to happen.

It was just like children playing in the playground, where one child just walks up to another and punches him in the face. It's not because the child is being malicious; he just wants to experience what it's like. And that's how it was. We were all so innocent, so pure, in a way. We were just children of God, out there playing and experiencing what it was like to create. But, during all this commotion and activity going on during the structuring of the Void into the dimensions, we began to notice something.

Everything was slowing down. From the moment that you might have wanted to consume another angelic being or interact with him, now there was a slightly delayed reaction, because all things in creation were beginning to slow down.

At first this was a relief because you had a little bit of time to respond and to feel into the experience. But, as time passed and things slowed down even more, angels began to talk about it. "Did you notice that things are really slowing down? If it continues at this rate, what will happen to all of us? Will we go out of existence? Will we stop being?"

Still, in spite of the concern that came over all of us, the groups of little angels became bigger and bigger, and the raiding parties, wars and attempts to steal energy began to intensify. Some even started to claim dimensions or territories as their turf, and the wars actually got to be quite large, quite grand.

The good thing was that it created a tremendous flow of energy for the construction of all of your dimensions and the physical universe. But it was also perhaps a bit naïve for us all to be doing this, because there could have been an easier way.

Star Wars

Eventually, various groups started banding together to protect and watch over each other, and to become stronger. There was still this underlying feeling that if enough angels got together, their combined energy and consciousness would be enough to bring them all back Home. But it never happened.

Eventually the angels began forming into very defined groups, and within the groups hierarchies began to form, with certain angels assigned to do certain things. In the end there turned out to be a total of 144,000 angelic or spiritual families.

At some point in all of creation, every angel took a vow to one of the 144,000 families. Some of the families were very, very large with billions of angelic beings. Some were quite a bit smaller, but it was the beginning of a type of society where souled beings gathered their energy together for the common good of all. Here we saw the alignment of energies with each of the 144,000 spiritual families. They started to work in specific areas or types of consciousness and became known as Orders – 144,000 Orders.

There were some who began to understand the need for peace, because their consciousness had grown to the point where they realized the wars didn't work, the fighting was a waste of energy, and the outcome was always the same. Of course, for a short period of time there might be some winners, but ultimately, there weren't. Ultimately, the hunger for power would actually work against those who were seeking it. The more the groups tried to take over other groups, the more susceptible they became to being taken over by yet a third group. And all this time things were slowing down. "How slow?" you ask. So slow that it started to create physical reality.

Physical reality is created when vibration or consciousness slows down to such a level that it becomes solid and defined, and now it was happening during this period that we call the "star wars," which was very similar to your movie series. In fact, the Star Wars movies are a depiction of what happened a long, long time ago: one group trying to take over the other, one group thinking they were better than another, but all groups trying to find the ultimate source.

Now, as angelic beings, we didn't fly around in little battleships. We melded our energies together and created a type of consciousness or thought-form. I guess it could be symbolized by little flying ships, but back then it was about melding our energy together.

It became quite distorted and perverted however, because what had been the original desire to go back Home had now become the desire for power. Home was all but forgotten. Some of these groups had but one mission – power – because it felt so good, but they didn't bother to realize that, ultimately, power was an illusion. That desire for power led to more desire for power and it ultimately became their undoing. But yet they were addicted to it. It was like a drug, and that's why we had all these galactic wars a long time ago.

The wars got very, very intense, and it could be perceived that they became very destructive. But, ultimately, you can't destroy a soul. Yes, you could shoot a soul off into another dimension, and that's what happened many times in these star wars. When one group would attack another, they found ways to blast each other into far-off dimensions. But an interesting thing happens: every souled being comes back. No matter how remote a dimension they're blasted to, something within returns them. It is a type of angelic rebirth that was discovered a long time ago – how to bring yourself back to the Now moment – and we did.

Still, during these very intense wars and collisions of energies and consciousness, things continued to slow down to the point that it got very frightening. The physical universe was now being manifested because of this slowed down energy, and we feared it was going to go too far.

Now, what you know as your physical universe is not quite as large as some scientists think. It is actually in a circular type of form, and scientists tend to use tools to measure time and space and a few other things that are not so accurate. But the physical universe was being created and there were souled beings and soul families who started going into this physical reality.

Their energy was so slowed down that they found themselves in the physical universe. They were not in bodies like you have now, but they found themselves energetically surrounding what were becoming the planets and solar systems and galaxies, and they began staking out these territories as their own.

Even today, when you look out into your physical universe, you can see the history and the old stories of some of these battles and explosions that took place. Among the non-physical beings there were fights and struggles for power and territory, and still things kept on slowing down and slowing down until it came to a near-critical stage.

You were there. You too were aware and concerned about what would happen next. You could feel that all of creation was coming to a standstill, and the question went out, from you and others of like consciousness, "Will we go out of existence if all expansion of consciousness comes to a halt? Will we go back into the Void if we stop expanding? Will all of creation collapse onto itself if things get so slow that they come to a standstill?"

Dear friend, take a deep breath.

You are an angel experiencing your own creations in what used to be the Void, but that is now filled with your expressions.

And so it was.

NOTES

NOTES

CHAPTER 6

ORDER OF THE ARC

And so it was that you asked the all-important question, "Who am I?" This single question launched you on a million times a million journeys, which have seemed to take eons of time, yet it's been only a breath since you first whispered those words. And since then, in this place that used to be the Void, creation has blossomed. It has given form and meaning and structure to what used to be nothing. In this time your soul, your divine essence, wrapped in a type of cocoon for protection and the inward look, has swelled. It has grown and expanded exactly as you chose it to do.

God-In-Training

The many external expressions of yourself, in a way, mean so very little. They are just experiences, and the soul understands them as wisdom, spiritual knowledge, and ways of coming to know the meaning of "I Am all that I Am." Any pain or wounds that these expressions have are not actually felt by the soul and the Spirit, for in its wisdom it knows that every experience is simply the discovery of who you truly are.

All this time, while you were interacting with the other angelic beings and forming your spiritual families, the soul has been growing and maturing. All this time your soul has been preparing for its own journey. Yes, it has been taking the deep inward look, but in time, in the right moment, it will take its journey to meet with you in a very real and very conscious way, no longer needing to be wrapped and protected, but joining you in the reality of your choosing.

And all this time, while the Void was being turned into an amazing creation by you and all of the other souled beings, back Home in the

Kingdom, the King and Queen have felt everything. They know every-thing. They haven't forgotten. While the memory of Home seems to have been erased or at least buried deep, deep within you, back Home the King and the Queen – Mother/Father God and All That Was – can still feel you. They know every thought, every emotion, every experi-ence that you have had, and their love is with you.

Out of love and compassion, they cannot and will not do it for you. They know that no matter what situation you give yourself, no matter how harrowing, difficult and dark, or how joyful and beautiful it may be, it is by your choice. And, because of their compassion, they do not interfere. They know that you are going to come through every experience as a grander being. They know that nothing can destroy the soul, that nothing can take away from you. They know that any experi-ence you have is yours by choice, at some level within you, and they honor and respect that. Therefore they do not interfere. They continu-ally send their love to you, and they continually receive what your soul is doing and how it's growing.

All this time, dear friend, in the Void, in the star wars, no matter where you have been or what you have done, you have been growing your own soul, preparing yourself for your sovereignty. You are God-in-training, learning the ways of creation and the ways of your Spirit.

Angelic Orders

So here you are, now aligned or affiliated with one of the 144,000 spiritual families, and these families are called Orders, because it is the first time in creation that some type of order is being established. No longer are you just little child angels on a vast playground, wildly playing and experimenting; now you are maturing. You're coming into your own, aligning and cooperating with others.

Through interacting with the other angelic beings, whether they are in your spiritual family or another, you are learning about yourself, and this is another grand gift of Spirit. If you had been the only souled being outside of All That Was, it would have been so much more difficult to learn and understand who you are. But, with these other children of God here with you, you are learning from them and they are learning from you. One of the joys of Spirit is to share, and you are sharing experiences, companionship, insights and wisdom. The others are like a mirror for you, and you are now beginning to see yourself in new and different ways.

Every souled being has their own journey, growing at their own pace and according to their own path. There is no prescribed group path, because every being progresses at their own pace, based on the desire of their own soul. It may seem that some are far, far behind, but that is an illusion, for there is no measurement of who's ahead and who's behind. It is that it is, and eventually all souled beings will find their sovereign place. They will come to understand that they're not going to find the answers in another souled being, or even in some book or through some other angelic being. Every souled being will discover that they are sovereign, and that they have all the answers and solutions within themselves. And every souled being is allowed to discover this in their own unique and absolutely brilliant way.

When you see a drunk or a destitute person along the side of the street, make no judgment on them, because they may be a very advanced soul, simply giving themselves the experience of losing everything. There are human souled beings who give themselves the experience of going into the very depths of darkness, not because they are weak or wrong, but because they have chosen to experience this in order to help answer the question, "Who am I?"

So the Orders, the spiritual families, were created, and it was amazing to watch, in spite of all of the battles and energy stealing, how souled beings could put their hearts and souls together and start working for a common good while still remaining absolute individuals. It was amazing how they could combine their creative energies to expand, grow, and learn.

These 144,000 Orders were the original spiritual families, and many of their names are still spoken in the human language today. The Order of Mika'el – Archangel Michael; the Order of Amael; the

Order of Metatron, now known as Yoham; the Order of Gabriel; the Order of Uriel – the names go on and on. And you, dear reader, have come from one of them.

These Orders were some of the first schools ever established in the angelic realms. They were places of learning, of coming to deep understandings about creation. Meditations were first done in some of these spiritual families. Understandings about the rejuvenation of energy and transmutation of consciousness were first developed in some of these laboratories of the spiritual families.

Each of the families took on their own unique attributes, and some began sharing and communicating with other families, teaching what they had learned. Underneath all of this interaction was still the desire to return back Home, but now it was also the desire to learn about Self, about the group or family, and about all of creation.

If you are reading this, you were among the leaders of these spiritual families. You were one who helped to gather the individual souled beings and organize these very first schools, these very first incubators of consciousness. You were also one who went out to try and help some of the lost souled beings who were wandering out in the other realms. You went out to help show them that there was a group or family that they could become part of in order to help them discover their own selves.

There are humans who come from all spiritual families, not just the Order of Mika'el or Hapiru or some of the others, and because you have been among the leaders and new thinkers of your own spiritual family, you helped to create the communication and the compatibility with the other spiritual families.

The Grandest Gathering
When all of the energies of creation began to slow down, there was a concern that if everything came to an absolute halt and consciousness stopped expanding, then creation would collapse on itself and everything outside of Home would go out of existence. So, the concern became "What happens?"

There were those who, using a type of spiritual mathematics, started plotting and measuring, projecting when everything would come to a halt. There were others who were working in what you would now call scientific developments, researching ways of how to reinvigorate the energy. But everything that was attempted seemed to have no success.

At last, nearing a critical mass of slowdown, the leaders of the spiritual families started connecting and communicating from their deepest soul level to other group leaders. Some of these groups were still very wounded from the battles that had taken place. Some had very large energetic walls or fortresses around them. Many of them were very anxious or nervous about interacting with any other spiritual families and had become very sequestered and hidden off by themselves because they felt it was safer to stay away.

Yet the call went out, from the leaders of one spiritual family to another, until all 144,000 families had been connected. And the leaders said, "We need to join our energies together for the common good, or we all potentially face extinction."

So it was that a grand gathering was called, and all of these spiritual families sent representatives to participate. It took a long time for planning, connecting and communicating between the leaders of all of these families, but eventually all agreed to join together in the first union of spiritual families. In this amazing gathering were represented all of the souled beings or all of the angels in creation.

Hundreds of representatives from each family were sent to this gathering, but only a few were chosen to speak on the behalf of each spiritual family. Every family had equal representation, based not on the size but on the uniqueness of that family.

This gathering of the families was the first common union of all beings, and it created a template that is still used today here on Earth. When there are crises, wars or global issues to be solved, this template is still followed today – the gathering of all of the representatives.

This gathering was called the Order of the Arc, because each spiritual family had developed an archetypical energy unique to them. The Order of Mika'el, for instance, was the archetypical energy of Truth. The Order of Amael was the archetypical energy of Hope, and the list goes on and on, and all of these families came together and discussed the situation.

And, dear one, if you are reading this right now, you were there at that gathering. Every being who is touched by this material, in one way or another, was there.

At this grand gathering there was a lot of discussion about the consequences of the slowdown, and also about how to get consciousness expanding again. And, of course, as you can imagine, there was a lot of argument and disagreement. A lot of different theories were put out, and all were accepted and listened to, with as little judgment on any one of them as possible.

Oh yes, because of the high energy in this Order of the Arc, sometimes it burst out into what you would now call emotions of anger, frustration and weariness, but it was known by all that some sort of resolution had to be developed.

Now, using a bit of a metaphor, all this time Spirit, back in the Kingdom, was watching and listening in on this gathering of the angels, this Order of the Arc. And in Spirit's heart there was joy, because Spirit was watching all the children of God now taking responsibility for themselves, working together for the common good, and working for their individual soul and expression as well. So you could say that on this day Spirit smiled, knowing that the angels were working on their own resolution.

The Plan of Hope

Many, many different ideas and theories were put forth, and ultimately 33 different plans were accepted. Each plan was different in its own right, and each plan was actually implemented. One of the plans was called the "Creation of Earth," and this plan was one of the most unique – and one of the riskiest – of all. But it also held some of the highest of hopes. And, in the Order of the Arc, implementing the plan of Earth was fairly simple.

The Order of the energy of Physical Manifestation, what you now call Gaia, would go to one of the planets in a solar system in a far, far off place that had not been subject to any of the wars in the physical universe and had not been affected by the energy battles. Gaia, an angelic being, would take a group of angels, go there, and embed the seed of life or consciousness on this far-away rock that you now call Earth. Gaia would breathe life itself into this rock, and that would eventually create the atmosphere, the air, the waters, and eventually the plants and the animals and all things that would sustain a certain type of physical life form.

So, as this plan was implemented, Gaia was called forth. And, in honor, representing her family and taking her angelic support team, Gaia descended through a very carefully constructed corridor down to this little place called Earth and began breathing life into it.

Part of the plan was that Earth would have very unique physical and energetic attributes so that no outsiders could interfere. If one of the spiritual families decided not to honor the agreement and try to attack this place called Earth, it would prove to be very, very difficult or nearly impossible to do. In this bubble of safety, Earth would become a grand experiment and a grand stage for acting out and resolving some of the issues that were taking place due to the energy slow-down.

Each of the other 32 plans were implemented as well, but it is the plan of planet Earth that we're talking about here, because this plan also required a large group of angels from each spiritual family to eventually reduce their vibration, descend down to Earth, take on physical form and take on the attributes of time and space. These angels would take on a physical body that would feel pain, as well as a mind that would allow them to maneuver on Earth.

The reason was quite simple. Earth would be a very protected environment where you would take on a physical form that would allow reality to slow down, but not go out of existence. It would allow the evolution to happen very, very slowly, so that the group of angels who had descended themselves to Earth would then be able to go back through all of the experiences they had ever had in the non-physical realms and reenact them, but now in physical reality.

Now, obviously, the stage that was set on Earth would make the reenactment quite a bit different than it had been in the other realms. But it would allow angels to battle once again, now in a very physical, very, very real way. It would allow them to steal energy from each other, but with very direct implications and very real consequences. It would allow the angels to go back through the experiences and actually feel what it was like to connect with or to love another angel as they had done in the non-physical realms, but now in this very real environment on Earth, because in this slowed-down reality they would be able to see the consequences. These angels would have the very conscious ability to make choices and then watch and realize how their choices were manifested. And this would eventually enable them to be more aware and conscious of their choices.

Earth was a place where the angelic beings could go to feel, reexperience and therefore understand what they had done in the angelic realms, but now in the very solid, very real, and very consequential theater of life.

Answering the Call

Now the big question was, who was going to go? The Order of Gabriel was called forth and asked to sound the metaphorical trumpet, calling angels from all of the spiritual families to be the first to go to Earth, to be the first wave. There were at least thirteen representatives from each spiritual family who were the first to come to Earth. Many, many more would follow later, but initially it was just this small group.

As exciting and adventurous as this may sound, those in the Order of the Arc couldn't guarantee what would happen. They couldn't guarantee that these angels would ever be able to return. Knowing the dynamics of Earth and its strong energetic pull, they didn't know if the angelic beings would get totally lost on Earth, if they would become so embedded in the physical reality that they may never get out. It simply wasn't known, so there was great risk in volunteering for this plan. And when Gabriel's call went out, there were many, many, many angels who backed away, wanting nothing to do with it.

However, there were a small number of angels, dedicated to All That Is, to the expansion of consciousness, and to releasing the slow-down of the expansion of All That Was Becoming, who stepped forward. Many of those who stepped forward were the very ones who were originally called to the Order of the Arc to help find the solution, and one of them was you.

You were already in the Order of the Arc. You already knew all of the plans and all of the consequences and all of the potentials for liberating consciousness, and you stepped forward. You were in the first wave of angels, or perhaps the second or third wave, but you stepped forward and said, "I will go."

Yes, there was a fear within, but there was also excitement. Indeed you had moments of wondering what you were doing and what you were possibly thinking, but above all, you had an overwhelming desire to go into this new experience, to go to this place of Earth and feel what it was like to take on physical form.

What an amazing reality it was! No longer just these "light thoughts" or airy feelings of non-physical reality. Now you could go into one of the deepest dimensions of all, and not only observe it but become embedded and embodied within it.

It is much like a painter who creates a beautiful painting and loves it so much that, instead of staying removed or outside the painting, decides to jump inside and become part of it. That's exactly what you did. You raised your hand and said, "I will go," and that, dear friend, is amazing service. That is being courageous and outrageous. And that is who you are.

You did it once, and you've done it many times since. You tend to be the first to go into new energies. You tend to be the explorer and adventurer, and yes, sometimes it tires you to the bone. Sometimes you wonder why you keep doing these things, why you keep going into these new energies and experiences, but that's who you are. And I ask you to love yourself for it, because you are at the forefront of creation. You are a true leader of your spiritual family.

Sometimes you diminish yourself. You think of yourself as just a lowly, inconsequential human. But I look you in the soul right now and I know who you are. I remind you that you're an adventurer, that you're outrageous, and that you love Spirit, your spiritual family and all angelic beings so much that you allow yourself to be the first into the new energies.

Farewell

So, you raised your hand and were among the first to go.

First, it was time to bid farewell to your spiritual family. You went back to them, met with them in counsel, and told them of your decision and of what you were doing. And they were amazed. They were in awe of you, as they have been for a very long time.

By the way, that's both a blessing and a curse. As a leader of your spiritual family, you tend to take on their issues as well as your own. You feel them watching over you, wondering how you're progressing, wondering how you're doing, because, ultimately, the success in freeing up your own consciousness and moving into your own sovereignty will determine some of their success. You're doing it first; they will follow. That's a phenomenal, amazing amount of responsibility, because it's going to be difficult to continue going forward while carrying the burden of your spiritual family any further.

So, you met with them and told them that you would be going to this place called Earth. You saw the love and emotion in their hearts. You saw the longing that they would have for you, and it was a very emotional moment when you bid them farewell, because you didn't know if you would ever see each other again. You had grown so close and connected, but you didn't know if you would ever be back with them again. At last, you bid farewell.

Returning back to the Order of the Arc, you met with the representatives from all of the angelic families who had helped develop the original plans for releasing this impasse of energy. And again, it was an emotional meeting. You were told of the potentials that you would face when you went to Earth – not that anybody really knew, but there were assumptions – because the energies were so seductive, so compelling, and it wasn't just the physical gravity. There was also a type of energy or spiritual gravity that would keep you on Earth for a long, long time.

They warned you of what it might be like to get so immersed into the energies that you would lose all touch with yourself. They told you that you would most likely forget about the Order of the Arc, your spiritual family, creation, and everything that you ever knew. You found it hard to believe that these energies of Earth could make you so easily forget, that you would come to the point of thinking you were only a limited human, totally forgetting that you were an angel.

And yes, this is was the dream that you had, back in the boat on the ocean of consciousness, the dream about being a grand soaring bird, an angel with beautiful wings, and suddenly growing small, suddenly turning dark, suddenly having the wings ripped right off of you. This moment was what you dreamt about. It was the warning from the angels of the Order of the Arc.

They told you that no matter what happened they couldn't rescue you. They would always be aware of you, of what you were doing and what your experiences were like, but they couldn't rescue you. First of all, it would negate the whole journey and defeat the whole purpose. And secondly, they could never get close enough to rescue you because they would be pulled in also.

You see, there's another important reason why Earth is never going to be subject to invasion from the aliens or from outer space forces. First of all, it is because Earth is, in a way, very well hidden from all of the other parts of the physical universe. Secondly, it is because the energies of Earth are so compelling that any alien being who got that close would be sucked into the Earth energies. Then they would have to take on human qualities and go through lifetime after lifetime of experience, just like you have. It would defeat their whole purpose of trying to take over Earth. So you could say Earth is a very unusual, but very safe place.

So, it was finally the eve of your departure from the Order of the Arc. You had prepared as much as possible for your journey to Earth, but there was little that you could actually do to prepare, because nobody knew what it would truly be like.

Gaia, who had gone to Earth to seed it with life energy, had never actually allowed herself to become embodied in the way that you would now be doing. Yes, part of her was deeply in Earth as part of the living essence of Earth, but part of her knew she would return at some point. It was true that part of her energies that helped to seed Earth had given you and all the others some clues of what it was like. But even she didn't understand all of the dynamics you would face.

All the representatives of the spiritual families of the Order of the Arc gathered together on that last night, that final moment together. It was sad, but it was also joyful. There was a feeling of tremendous bravery and courage, and there were also your personal feelings of weakness, uncertainty and doubt. There was admiration in the eyes and the hearts of all the other angels who weren't going, and a deep bonding among the angelic beings who would be the first to depart.

Then, preparing to descend to Earth, you took that final breath in the Order of the Arc.

You breathed in and savored all of the energies of yourself, feeling how much you had grown and learned over this long, long time in what used to be the Void.

You breathed in the energies of your spiritual families and all the ones who you had come to know and love.

You breathed in the energies of all of the angels you had ever tried to consume and all of the ones you had battled with.

You breathed in one last breath on the other side.

And so it was.

NOTES

NOTES

CHAPTER 7

COMING TO EARTH

And so it was that the energies of the Order of Gaia went to this small rock in some far-off distant place in the physical universe, and began to breathe life into it.

Time

It is said that in human measurement terms this Big Bang occurred approximately nine billion years ago. Perhaps, just perhaps, the Big Bang is when you went through the Wall of Fire. Perhaps it is still seen out there somewhere in the cosmos, this explosion of energy and consciousness as you went from the First Circle, from All that Was, into the Void, into your new playground, into this gift that Spirit had given you to go and explore and create within.

It is said that this place of Earth is approximately 4.5 billion years old, and that life on Earth is somewhere around 2.5 to 3 billion years old. But as we take this next part of our journey of the angels, now coming to Earth, understand that time, the way humans measure it right now, is not very accurate. Time is actually not linear and consistent, unless, of course, you wear a wristwatch and flip the pages of a calendar each day. In reality, time has its own type of movement.

In the angelic realms, "time" is actually measured by a sequence of events. Or, perhaps better stated, it is measured by the expansion of consciousness. So time, in the non-physical realms, is sometimes very compressed, sometimes very stretched out. There have been moments in history where time actually wraps around itself, sometimes loops in and out of itself. Sometimes the waveform of time is very consistent, other times very, very erratic.

So, if you want to put a human measurement on the age of Earth, you could say it is approximately 4.5 billion years old. But for the angelic beings coming here and beginning their adventures on Earth, time is basically irrelevant. It doesn't really matter. Although you measure it now by your instruments and by the sun coming up each day, that is very, very artificial. So, for now, we're going to ask you to suspend the human interpretation of time and allow the more authentic elements of time as a sequence of events and the expansion of consciousness to come in.

In a way it could be said that everything that has happened since you left Home and went through the Wall of Fire was only a breath ago. To you, a human sitting here reading this, it may seem like so very long ago that you left Home. But in a very real way it was just a breath ago.

The Order of the Arc

The Order of Gaia, the ones that are responsible for breathing new life into creation, came to this place called Terra or Earth, at the request of the Order of the Arc.

The Order of the Arc is still in existence today. It contains 144,000 "pillars" or symbols, one for each of the angelic families. The Order of the Arc is truly what is keeping everything together, from a consciousness standpoint, in the non-physical realms. It is an agreement or a type of concurrence among all the spiritual families, because at the core they all have a very similar agenda – the expansion of consciousness. They all want to go beyond this slowdown of consciousness, for they do not want to have to face what happens if everything comes to an absolute standstill.

The Order of the Arc has been a beautiful thing. It is called the "Arc" because it is made up of archetypical or representative energies from all of the angelic families. Every angel who is here in human form can draw upon the strengths and attributes of each of the various archetypical energies. They are here to support you and to be a nurturing place during your journey on Earth, and you can call them forth at any time.

There is not the time or space here to go through what each Order represents. Perhaps some will be inspired to begin feeling into the energies of each of these Orders or angelic families and begin writing down or documenting some of the various names and their supporting or archetypical energies.

The Order of the Arc is here to support you. It doesn't make your decisions for you, it doesn't do any healing for you, but you can draw on its many strengths, because they are your strengths also.

Oneness

It is also called the Order of the Arc because there is literally an arcing energy stretching from one angelic family to another, almost like a light arc that has connected all of the families together. Oftentimes, when humans talk about oneness of all of creation, they are actually tapping into these arcs that unite together all of the spiritual families into a type of oneness.

We're also going to make another point here about oneness. In the beginning you indeed came from Oneness. However, when you went through the Wall of Fire and took on your own soul, you truly became your own One. As we have said earlier, you never go back Home. You never go back into a homogenous oneness. You go forth into discovering that you are your own One.

In understanding your own oneness, you begin to understand the commonality with every other souled being, the fact that you all came from the First Circle. You also develop the compassion and understanding that each and every souled being will become – or already is – sovereign in their own right. Each souled being becomes their own One, but you never go back into a communal oneness. That would be like rejecting the gift of Spirit, for Spirit has given you the gift of your own oneness and is asking you to go forth and fulfill it.

Indeed, take a deep breath with that.

Breathing Life into Earth

Gaia came to this rock called Earth and began breathing the energies of life into it. By the way, you too can breathe your consciousness into any object, such as a rock. With the purity within you and a focus of your own consciousness, you can breathe your life into anything – something you make out of clay, a painting that you're going to put on the wall – anything. You can breathe your life into it and it begins to have its own living aspect.

So, Gaia, on behalf of the Order of the Arc, breathed life into this rock called Earth. Gaia, with all of the supporting angels who accompanied her, brought life to Earth, and it took a long, long time, if measured by your current human terms. But, in a way, it was just a breath ago that life was brought to this rock.

Preparing Earth for your eventual arrival, and with the support of other angelic Orders, Gaia created a passageway or tunnel from the Order of the Arc down to Earth. In a very real way, it was a one-way tunnel, for it would be the doorway that you would eventually use to descend your energy down to Earth. Later on, there would be many different tunnels, and much later on there would be other types of vortexes or tunnels that would lead out to the non-physical realms surrounding Earth. But for right now, a single one-way tunnel was built.

Then, Gaia breathed in the elements of this planet Earth. She breathed in air. She breathed in water. She breathed in terra, or the earth itself, that would cover the surface of this rock. And she breathed in fire, which would become a transmutational energy, as well as provide for rejuvenation and renewal. The energy of fire would also provide for the release of Spirit energy that would become embedded in solid matter.

After these basic elements had been breathed into this rock called Earth, Gaia breathed in the primary kingdoms of Earth that are still here. She breathed in the kingdom of the forests and the plants. She breathed this in to sustain life force energy on Earth, for your trees, shrubs, plants and grasses are all ways of sustaining living energy on

Earth; they are all here to support you. The kingdom of the plants and trees was also placed here for nourishment, because there had to be some way to sustain the physical body. And by eating these plants that were breathed into Earth, it would sustain the physical biological body that you would eventually take on.

In the beginning it was intended that all biological forms, all animals and eventually humans would eat of this plant kingdom on Earth. It was put here as your garden, as nourishment for the physical body that you would eventually take on. It wasn't until much, much later that animals and humans began to eat the meat and the flesh

Gaia breathed in the energies of the water and all of the beings that were in the water, particularly the waters that contained the salts, because this was going to be important to maintain biological balance on Earth. Right now, on its surface, Earth is approximately two-thirds water and one-third land, and the waters are very, very important, for a wide variety of scientific reasons, but also for spiritual reasons.

The saltwater in particular constantly helps to absorb what you would call negative, congested or polluted energies, and this happens on a continual basis even if you don't live near the ocean. The saltwater on Earth is constantly helping to absorb some of the stuck or negative energies of humanity and cleanse them in a very brilliant and beautiful way. That is why, when you've had intense experiences or when you're feeling run down, we often suggest bathing yourself in saltwater, because it helps to bring out and absorb some of these negative energies.

Gaia breathed in the animals and fishes that would be in the oceans, and to this day these creatures also serve a very important purpose in helping to maintain the delicate balance of Earth. Beyond being used now for a food source, the balance of the aquatic life is also very, very important for maintaining a constant flow and rebalancing of energies on Earth.

Gaia also breathed in the animal kingdom and all of its potentials. In the beginning there were not a lot of different types of animals, though eventually there would be many, many species, and the animals were also brought in to maintain a balance of the life force energies on Earth.

Another reason the animals were breathed into Earth is because they would provide the template or the basic forms for what would eventually become the human body. You would be coming to Earth, eventually associating or relating your energy to the animal beings, and then the human species would eventually develop from that.

Gaia also breathed in the energies of the devic or the fairy kingdom. These are all of the little non-physical beings who are also responsible for maintaining a balance between the physical and non-physical realms of Earth. Some of you can see them, particularly at night, if you go off into the meadows and forests. These beings are constantly shifting and shuttling energies back and forth between the animal and plant kingdoms and are responsible for maintaining that incredible balance. They actually make the plants, trees and animals sing and they have to maintain the harmony among of these different life forms on Earth. These beings have been very, very active and a very important part of the development and growth of the physical Earth.

The elemental beings are now starting to leave, because their job is done. There will always be some of these fairy energies on Earth, but humans are beginning to take more and more responsibility for this planet. So now a lot of Gaia's energies in the fairy kingdom are being released.

Gaia also breathed in the energies of the crystalline kingdom on Earth. Now, here "crystalline" doesn't necessarily mean the physical rocks and crystals of Earth but rather a crystalline or birthing type of energy. The crystalline energies were particularly important in the very early days of Earth, and Gaia breathed them deep, deep into the Earth.

The crystalline energies have been very important for maintaining a type of balance between the physical and the non-physical realms. They contained tremendous energies that you used when you came to Earth, energies that allowed the transmutation of your angelic consciousness into the physical Earth.

You may have a love for crystals even now, and this is because many of them still contain a trace of that original crystalline energy. Most of that energy is gone now because humans have learned to take more and more responsibility for Earth, but yet there is still that cellular memory within you of the pure, light-form crystalline energies that were put into the rocks, into the soil, and deep within the Earth.

Even to this day, at the center of Earth itself, there is a huge crystalline energy. Don't think of it in terms of a big rock but rather a type of light energy that is still there. Oh yes, it's surrounded by all this molten lava and heat and everything else that you know about Earth, but at its very core there is still an incredible crystalline energy. It still communicates with some of the remaining crystals on Earth. It communicates with the animal kingdom and the fairy kingdom and the aquatic kingdom, sending out a constant type of tone or frequency, helping to maintain this very, very delicate balance on Earth.

When Gaia breathed in the crystalline energies on Earth, she also breathed in many of the potentials and keys to unlock certain parts of human consciousness as it developed, and they are still held in many parts of the Earth. They are like keys that you use to open up and activate certain things within your physical and your non-physical being along your journey to enlightenment.

These are not what you would call secrets, and they are not the answer in themselves. They are reminders to you, placed along the path of your awakening, reminding you to allow things like the changing of your DNA process. It is partly activated from within you through your conscious choice, but because you are a biological being, it is also co-activated by some of these crystalline energies still in the Earth.

Perhaps you wonder sometimes why you feel called to go to a certain place on Earth, without really knowing why? It may be the internal calling from within you to be at a place where there is a higher potential for the activation of crystalline energies from the Earth itself into you. You don't need to stay there for weeks or months of time, sometimes just being in that direct energy for a short time provides the trigger for your own DNA. Sometimes you've experienced crystalline energies in strange or unusual places, and that is also helping to unlock the limitations of the human mind by triggering a process. Again, the crystalline keys of Earth aren't actually the secrets, but they are helping to activate and begin a process within you that relates to your physical journey here on Earth.

So it was that Gaia breathed all of these beautiful energies into Earth and agreed to stay very closely associated with the living essence of Earth for a long, long time, until the humans began to take responsibility for their own journey on Earth. She has been here from the beginning, and now, slowly, her energies are starting to leave so that humans can take on the responsibility for this planet.

A Final Farewell

When the energies of Earth were balanced and ready to support the angelic beings, the call went out once again, alerting all of those – including you – who had agreed to come, that the time was right.

Perhaps you can remember that last moment in the Order of the Arc, surrounded by representatives of all of the spiritual families, nobody knowing for sure what was going to happen, nobody knowing how this particular one of the 33 plans was going to work out. But there was something inside you that did know.

You could sense so much of your upcoming journey. You could sense that this had the highest potential to allow the expansion of consciousness. Something inside you also knew that this was going to be a very challenging and difficult journey, that it was going to feel like you were very, very lost at times. But there was something deep within you that knew you were going to come through it, that knew you were going to awaken something within yourself that would also help to awaken something in all of the rest of creation.

So many of us remember that moment so very, very well, that final moment in the Order of the Arc, surrounded by love and compassion, anxiety and fear. And in that last moment together, we took a breath, together with the angelic beings of the Order of the Arc, and they reminded you, as once Spirit had reminded you, that you would never be alone; that the angels of all the angelic families would be there in love and support; and while it may seem at times like you were totally out of contact, they would always have you in their hearts.

At last you took that final breath in the Order of the Arc, and allowed yourself to plunge into the tunnel, into that pathway that had been created by the energy of Gaia. You let go, surrendered, and allowed yourself to start descending down into this place called Earth.

The Tunnel

In a way it was very much like going back into the Wall of Fire. It was very confusing, very disorienting. You felt yourself spinning and turning and tossing, but now, instead of being shattered into billions and billions of pieces, you had a new experience. You felt like you were being absolutely compressed and squeezed, like you were being suffocated and closed within.

At this point it would have been a relief to feel a shattering, because the energies were becoming denser and tighter and more compacted. You wanted to break out from them and open up, but you only felt them squeezing, tightening, pushing and compacting you.

You wanted to scream out, open up, release, but the energies just got denser and stronger. You resisted and fought against the compression. It was a natural reaction, but the more you resisted, the more the energies tightened and compacted and pushed and pushed and pushed.

Now you felt something very akin to physical pain. You screamed out, wanting it to end, yet it seemed endless.

As you were being compressed tighter and tighter, you tried to remember the Order of the Arc. You tried to remember the angels who were bidding you farewell, but even that memory was being squeezed out of you.

You felt a type of a suffocation. You felt your own spirit being extinguished as you drew closer and closer to the non-physical realms of this planet Earth.

The more you resisted, the more it seemed to push at you, squeeze you, and pull you in even deeper. Even to this very day you still have dreams about what it was like to be in that passageway leading from the Order of the Arc to Earth, feeling out of control, plunging into darkness, having the life squeezed out of you, going from feeling very expanded and light to feeling very compressed and dark and small and restricted.

Arrival

After what felt like an endless journey through this corridor, suddenly everything seemed to open up. There was light once again, but a light like you'd never seen before. You felt a bit of expansion, a bit of opening, and suddenly you took a deep breath – the first breath you had been able to take in a long, long time, the first breath since leaving the Order of the Arc – and to your absolute amazement you were now a non-physical being on Earth.

In a way, it was very similar to being on an airplane. You're high above the clouds and then you plunge down through them; everything becomes a bit confusing, you lose track of where you are, and then suddenly you dive down beneath the cloud layer and it unveils and reveals Earth itself. What a beauty.

Now, you didn't have a physical body or physical senses at that point, but you could sense a light like you'd never seen or experienced before. It was coming from the sun and shining on Earth, and it was amazing. You were in absolute awe of what Gaia had created for you.

You could sense the blueness of the ocean, the green of the land, the density of the air. And while part of you was still trying to work against it, trying to crawl back up through the tunnel you had just come through – because it was indeed a frightening experience – this other part of you, the adventurer that you are, was in total awe of what you beheld.

This was a Kingdom. This was your new playground. This was a spectacular expression of physical reality, and you allowed yourself now, through taking the deep breaths, to descend your energy closer and closer to Earth.

You were still a non-physical being and it was still very, very uncomfortable to be so tightly compressed and condensed. But yet you were also in absolute awe and amazement. You had never seen a plant before. You had never seen so much water before. And now you began playing on Earth.

Discovering Eden

Initially, you weren't aware of any other angelic beings because you were so captivated by these things that you would come to know as trees. Earth had developed over billions of years, becoming a beautiful garden, and here you were in it, experiencing it for the first time.

When your energy was fully descended, the first thing you did was take those deep non-physical breaths and allow yourself to absorb the colors, the light, the living essence of Earth itself. Through taking the deep breaths you also connected yourself to the crystalline energies, as well as to the energies of each one of the kingdoms of Gaia.

In human terms you could say this lasted a long, long time, where you just allowed yourself to breathe and absorb, but it was only the breaths that counted, not so much the "time." You breathed in the energies of the water. You breathed in the energies of the plants and the trees. You breathed in the energies of the animals, large and small. What an amazing playground.

After this breathing, which would be measured in a long, long span of human time, after fully and absolutely absorbing the energies of Earth itself, you began your playtime, your discovery time. Now, instead of just breathing in the energies, you let yourself flow your own energy right into the tree. As a non-physical type of light-form energy, you allowed yourself to flow into the tree and just be the tree, feeling what it was like to be dense and alive at the same time. You would let your energy be with that tree, and the tree, being in service to you, allowed you to become part of it and feel its essence, its life flow energy.

You would allow yourself to flow into the rocks of Earth, to feel what it was like to be that dense and solid. Yes, even rocks have consciousness and they welcomed you into them and let you be part of them. They don't have the same type of life flow energy as a tree, but yet there is life even within a rock, and you let your energy become part of it. You could feel the breath of Gaia that helped to create it.

You discovered the devas and the fairies, the non-physical beings, and you felt such an affinity and close partnership with them. You let the fairies and the devas take you around, floating from flower to flower, tree to tree. They showed you the ways of the devic kingdom, and you became very close to them. Perhaps it could be said that you spent eons of time doing this, but time didn't matter, and actually it still doesn't.

You began to know all the different forms and families of the fairy kingdom, and they let you become part of them, allowing your energies to flow into them and theirs into you. There was no holding back, there was no fear and no resistance. You just let yourself float with them and become part of the Earth.

Then you let yourself become part of the waters. Whether saltwater, oceans, lakes, or clouds, you let yourself become part of the consciousness of water. You let yourself drink in the energies of the water, and it felt so soothing to your light body.

The waters showed you how they flowed, how they rejuvenated and cleansed. The waters showed you how they helped balance the physical biological life forms of Earth. You learned from the waters, and you spent ages of time just being water.

Eventually you let your energies and consciousness flow into the animal kingdom, letting yourself become part of the animals and birds of Earth. And yes, the animal forms back then looked different, but yet with many similarities to the ones you know now.

You allowed yourself to simply ride along with them, flowing your energies into them, feeling what you would eventually know as a heartbeat, feeling life force energy flow through the body, feeling what it was like to eat of the plant forms of Earth to provide nutrition for the physical body. You spent eons of time playing with the many different animals, melding your energies with theirs, but above all you found such joy and comfort with becoming part of the fish of the oceans, lakes and seas of Earth. You developed such a close bond with what you now know as the dolphins and whales. Although they looked a little different, they indeed existed even back then, for Gaia had breathed this type of life form into Earth.

You loved flowing with them because the combination of the biology form with the water energies was so soothing. At times it was still very painful and stressful to be this attached to physical reality, but being with the dolphins and the whales soothed your light body. You found it to be much more natural and flowing than with some of the other animals of Earth, and you developed a close relationship with the whales and dolphins that exists even today.

Sometimes you have dreams of going back out into the ocean. And indeed you have had many, many lifetimes where you chose to be on the ocean, even when you were in the human form, becoming a sailor or a merchant on the oceans, because those energies are still so rejuvenating and soothing to you.

Birth

And so it was that you spent eons of time in your light body, exploring this playground of Earth. You were getting closer and closer to the crystalline energies, the energies of Earth and all of its kingdoms, until you knew them inside and out. You knew how life force energy flowed. You knew how the biology worked. You understood the natural decomposition and rebirth process on Earth, and you were loving it.

You got closer and closer to the animal kingdom of Earth, until one day you had become such a natural part of creation and had come in so close that you were actually birthed into biological body. It doesn't matter what your first life form looked like, whether it was from the aquatic kingdom or the animal kingdom. What matters is you had gotten so attached to physical form that you were actually birthed.

This is significant because until then you had always just ridden along or flowed in with the physical reality and the physical elements. But now you were actually birthed into a biological form. It was an amazing experience – feeling your angel energies go through the gestation process and the physical birth – and now you were here, part of the biological life on Earth. No longer just a free spirit flowing into the waters and plants and devic forms on Earth, now you were part of Earth in a biological, physical body.

It was an amazing experience, feeling this connected, but yet it was also frightening because now you were committed. You were no longer just the observer or the outsider, you were part of Earth. And in this precious moment you had a very deep knowingness that it was going to be a long, long journey in physical form on Earth, a long journey of being a part of biological life, a part of Earth itself, and a long, long time before you would ever be released from biology.

To this day, this is a very, very important trauma point, because there has been a resistance and anger, as well as a love and acceptance of being here. At times you love being human, here on Earth in physical form, and at times you feel it is the greatest prison that you have ever created for yourself.

When you were birthed into biological form there was also more forgetting of where you came from, forgetting the Order of the Arc, forgetting your angelic families, forgetting Home itself. Now you were a part of Earth, and all the memories of your journey up to now were dissolving away. Now your angelic energy was very tightly focused on Earth and in biology, and when you took that first breath as a physical being you felt the constriction of being trapped and totally immersed within creation.

Some time today – today, in your Now day – go out in nature, alone; just you and nature. The very best time is at sunset, where you have the combination of all the elements. Be in nature. Go hug a tree. Breathe in the air. If possible, be near water or at least connect with the water. Allow yourself to connect with the animal kingdom. Bring your dog if you have one. Otherwise, just feel the animal kingdom. Connect with the birds in the sky. Feel the essence of Gaia once again.

The memories are so deep within you of when you were an angelic being just floating around and connecting to all of these energies, and now you have become these energies. Go out today in nature and understand that, as much as you have been a part of all of these energies, you are soon going to be releasing yourself from them.

Indeed, you will always carry the memories of your time on Earth, but you're approaching the Point of Separation of releasing yourself back out of physical form.

Take a few moments today and connect back into Gaia, back into nature, because it is an intimate part of you.

Take a deep breath and rejoice for your experience in biology.

And so it was.

NOTES

NOTES

CHAPTER 8

LEMURIA AND ATLANTIS

And so it was, dear friend, as we begin this chapter, I would like to speak for a moment about life in the human body. There is nothing like it. Yes, it's difficult at times because you feel so lost. You want to remember your past lives to help you recreate your identity but count your blessings, for there are times when it is good that you don't remember. Sometimes the memories of past lives can tend to overshadow the current lifetime, and this lifetime is so very important.

Being human is difficult because sometimes you feel lost and disconnected from Spirit, from your own source and divinity, but you never truly are. You can reestablish that connection whenever you're ready to invite your divine into your life. It's not about going out into some other dimension or galaxy to reunite with yourself, but rather creating that beautiful safe space, your energetic Home, right here on Earth. When you prepare that Home within yourself and allow your divine to join you here, that's when you reconnect in a very conscious way with your Self.

The Blessings of Life as a Human

There are many humans who think that when you cross over and go to the other side, everything is perfect. They think that the angels have better music, better food, better sex, or whatever else it happens to be, but I'm here to tell you that there is nothing like being a human. It is the ultimate experience for any angel – as long as you're allowing yourself to enjoy life.

There is nothing at all like human music. It has far more depth and compassion than angelic music, which tends to be a little bit airy. Human music tells the journey of your human experiences.

Human food and nutrition goes directly into the body and feeds it. In the other realms you could say we just eat light, and that's not nearly as much fun as when you can really digest the food and feel that life force essence coming into your body.

When you're a human you can touch another person. When two angels meld together, yes, it is a beautiful experience, but it is nothing like touching the flesh of another human.

Angelic conversations are wonderful. We don't use language like you do, it's more a type of universal resonance. But when you get into your human languages, if you were to listen beyond the words, there is incredible depth and emotion and feeling in them that goes beyond just the language itself.

Truly, the angels in the other realms can't wait to come into human form. They've heard all the stories from you and other angels who have been here, and they can't wait to have this experience. And yes, perhaps the experience will be easier for them because of the path you have blazed in your own journey.

So, let us get back to the history of creation.

Being in Biology

So now you have been birthed into biological form. It is an amazing miracle – taking spirit energy and birthing it into biology – but also quite harrowing, because you knew in a very deep part of you that you were here now. You were committed to the program. You couldn't just float around anymore, moving yourself and your energy into trees and animals. You were fully here.

We call this first era of humanity the Lemurian era. It lasted for millions and millions of years, but again, remember that time is of little consequence. When you start trying to measure everything in timeframes, particularly if those timeframes are not true measurements, you tend to go very mental and then you forget the essence of your incarnations on Earth.

Here also is a perfect opportunity to begin letting yourself remember your past. You don't want to cling onto your other lifetimes, but allow yourself to remember the essence of what it was like to start integrating into biology.

As you allow yourself to remember, you're going to get glimpses and feelings. Remember not to take them terribly literal, because sometimes you'll just get symbolic interpretations. But they're going to start coming through because these are aspects or parts of you. Lifetimes are creations of your soul.

Many of these aspects have integrated back into you. Some are waiting for this opportunity right now. You don't have to remember every detail of a past life, what name you had or even what nationality. Let yourself remember and feel the essence.

We are working with you right now, in this moment, to help bring back some of the memories of these past lives. Just take a deep breath, stop worrying about the details, and the remembrance will come back to you, if not right now, in the days and months ahead.

It's time for you, at this point in your spiritual journey, to start remembering. It is also time to trust yourself in what you feel, because these have been beautiful experiences. You have the spiritual maturity now to remember them without getting distracted or overwhelmed by the emotion or the particular agenda or contract from that lifetime. Let yourself start remembering who you have been, and the essence of your experiences.

So, these first lifetimes in biological form were an absolute thrill, but also very challenging. It was – to use a human analogy – like trying to ride a wild horse without a saddle and without using your hands. Here you were, trying to integrate into a physical biological body, but yet there was a big part of you that was resistant. It felt uncomfortable and unnatural on one hand, and exciting and exhilarating on the other.

Here in biology you could actually start to use what would later develop into your human senses of sight, smell, hearing, taste and feel – something you weren't really able to do before – and it was amazing. It was expansive and deep.

Imagine for the first time looking out through the physical eyes of your host biology rather than just through your spiritual eyes. You see, spiritual eyes enable you to see what we call vibrational value, but biological eyes offer a whole different perspective. Allow yourself to remember peering out through physical eyes for the first time. It gave a whole new meaning to life.

Allow yourself to remember the first time, still struggling to adjust to this biological body, of being able to feel through the skin of that biological being that you had been birthed into. Remember the first times of feeling the sensations of heat and cold, feeling them like an angel can never do. Remember feeling pain at a very intimate level, a physical pain that told you instantly that you were in biology and you were very much alive, as uncomfortable as it was.

Remember being able to smell, experiencing this great gift of smell you had given yourself. You were no longer just feeling the essence of the forests and the animals and the water, but now able to smell saltwater, one of the earliest impressions that you had. Or to smell a flower, and then taste it and eat it.

That first time you ever took a bite of food or tasted your mother's milk – how it seemed to explode within your biology, rejoicing and singing and bringing life into your biology.

Remember being able to hear the sounds of nature, like an angel can never do – the singing of birds, the wind through the grasses and trees, the sounds of the waters – bringing whole new dimensions to your experience.

So, while it was very difficult adjusting into biology, it was also an amazing experience that, at a cellular level, you will never forget. In fact, that's one of the things that has brought you back to Earth again and again – the pure joy of your physical senses.

And still, it was very difficult adjusting into this biology. There was a resistance to it, not so much on the part of your biological carrier or your physical body, but you weren't sure how to meld your own spirit energy into it. You had practiced before, but now you were here, you were in, and there was still a part of you that kept trying to reject the body.

Creating the Near Earth Realms

So, very quickly, you experienced the next important phase of being in biology: death. Sometimes it was a painful death, because in trying to ride this wild biological body that you were in, you did strange things to it like falling off a cliff or drowning yourself because you forgot to breathe before you went under water. These were all things that you had to learn along the way!

So now you experienced death, and actually, the first death was the easiest death you ever had. You've had difficulty ever since, but the first was easy – you were in the body and suddenly the next moment you were out – and now an interesting thing happened. Where were you? What happened when you died?

Obviously, the spirit continues to exist, but you couldn't go back Home, and initially you couldn't even go back to the energies of your spiritual families. It would take a long time before those corridors or portals were developed that allowed you to go back and visit your angelic families in between lifetimes. This is something, by the way, that very few humans do, even though the pathway is there.

So now you found yourself suspended in spirit form again, and suddenly you began to realize you weren't alone. Now, we're going to define this new place you were in as the Near Earth realms. In other words, they are not physical but are still extremely connected to Earth and have many of the attributes and remembrances of Earth such as gravity and density, just without a physical body.

So here you were, surrounded by the spirit forms of trees and other animals that had died, existing in a kind of suspended state. So, you got together and, in a manner of speaking, compared notes with each other about that first life in physical form.

Those connections that you started making with the other non-physical beings at this point now started to create a natural structure that began to expand the Near Earth realms. Eventually these would become very, very complex, but right now you found a common place, along with the other newly dead ones who had just crossed over, and together you created a dimension within the Near Earth realms where beings would start going in between lifetimes. It was like a waiting room, a discussion room, and in this space you would wait for your next incarnation.

Sometimes you would go immediately back into the physical biology; other times you would wait what you would now call hundreds or thousands of years before your next incarnation. But in those realms, it doesn't make a difference.

These Lemurian times were quite beautiful. There weren't many wars. There wasn't a lot of energy stealing. It was a time of the peaceable kingdom, of angels getting familiar with the physical body.

You began to experiment and play with different types of physical incarnations, for there were no human forms at that time, nothing that you would now equate to the human body. You would choose a lifetime as a winged being to experience what that was like. Next, you might choose to be a dinosaur type of being – huge, clumsy and very hungry – and you would allow your energy to be birthed into this form. Sometimes, by the way, in those types of animal beings back then, you could live to be hundreds and hundreds of years old.

Then, after the death of that physical being, in between lifetimes you would go to these Near Earth realms once again, bringing all the wisdom, experience and information that you had gained in that incarnation. There was a lot of sharing between the angelic beings, especially about how to stabilize yourself in a physical form, because that was very challenging. There was a part of you that just kept wanting to pop out, a part of you that felt very awkward being confined into biology.

At this point there was very little brain structure in any of these biological forms that you were taking on, because it was essentially about living through the senses. You didn't have a human-type brain like what you have now, but you were developing the physical senses and letting yourself experience.

The Joy of Biology

I, Tobias, remember many of my own lifetimes, and I loved coming to Earth in the Lemurian times and taking on the form of all these different types of animals and fish and everything from tiny little insects to huge elephant type animals. And one of the things I loved more than anything else was to eat. I just loved to eat and I would go back to Earth again and again just to eat.

There wasn't a lot of drama or conflict with the other beings – we were all far too occupied with just learning to adjust into biology – but we loved to find specialized types of plants and trees and learn to eat the leaves and berries. There were certain kinds of fruits on Earth back then that cannot be found now, and I loved eating them because they were so sweet. I would just eat and eat and eat until sometimes I ate myself to death, went to the other side and shared my stories with many of you. I got so fat on Earth! I was such a glutton that I killed myself – and I couldn't wait to go back and do it again!

In the early days of Lemuria, all of the biological beings were what you would call asexual. A being would have the ability to create its own offspring and there was no need to have sex. Well, that got boring, so eventually, and also as a way of bringing in the masculine-feminine energy duality, we started to separate the energies. And, over the millions and millions of years of the Lemurian era, the animal species evolved into having both the masculine and the feminine expression. Now, that's when it really got to be fun – being birthed into biology as one or the other, and then being able to have sex.

So, when I gave up my gluttony after all those lifetimes of eating all the time, then I began to have sex all the time. And it was amazing in some of these various forms. Now if we were to tell stories about that, you might almost be ashamed of yourself – and of me! – but the important point is that we were allowing ourselves to experience life. And all of this development was helping to stabilize our angel energy in the biological form.

There were species on Earth back then that don't exist today, and that is appropriate. Sometimes you worry about the loss of a species on Earth, but there is no need to be concerned. Certain species stay for certain periods of time, in service to Earth and to humans, and then they leave. You notice right now on Earth in your current era that there are species leaving, but there are also amazing new species coming in.

So, back to our story. As we compared notes in the Near Earth realms between lifetimes, we started to focus in on certain types of species that served our spirit energy better. Again, the whales and dolphins were a natural choice, and there is still an amazing connection between humans and these aquatic forms.

In fact, I would go so far as to say there are still angelic beings who decided never to go beyond those forms. There are still angels in the form of dolphins, whales and a few other species, because they so loved those forms. They didn't care that the rest of us moved on, and they've actually served a very important function to help maintain a balance and a connection to the animal kingdom.

Perfecting Biology

We began to focus in on certain types of species to begin refining them for the purpose of carrying our spirit energy. We found that certain species were better adapted to the refinement of the physical senses, while other species really didn't suit us so well. Eventually we developed about seven different types of prototypical biological structures, and, as we were doing so, we were also developing the DNA, cells, organs and eventually the brains of those particular species. The many other species, of course, were here simply to serve Gaia and to serve us.

These were amazing times, but they weren't perfect, as some like to think of the Lemurian era. We were still struggling in the body, but now, instead of knowing death to be a natural part of the evolution process, we actually started resisting death, which then made it more difficult. And, of course, all this time we had forgotten who we really were. Yes, there would be a certain awareness, particularly when we crossed over into the other realms at death, but we were forgetting more and more about who we were and how we got here.

But these were amazing times indeed, and I invite you to open yourself up to some of the memories of the times in Lemuria. You'll begin to understand, also, why you have a certain affinity to different types of animals.

The birds, which I dearly love, were such a wonderful life form, and were indeed one of the seven different structures that we were developing. There was a point when many of us thought that birds would be the final form we would take, but alas, we wanted to be down closer to Earth, so eventually we chose what was to become the human form you know now.

Standardization in Atlantis

Let's move forward in time now to the next era, which we call the Atlantean era. Now, there wasn't a specific point of delineation here. In other words, we didn't cross over in a single day from Lemuria to Atlantis. As a matter of fact, these societies coexisted for hundreds of thousands of years, side by side, in different geographical parts of the world.

But Atlantis was basically founded as one of the first true communities on Earth. Up until then we had simply been many different species. We could recognize each other as a souled being inhabiting a physical body versus just a regular animal, because a souled being has a type of glow around them. There is a very special aura around a souled being, so back in Lemuria it was very easy to tell if some type of animal or bird was a souled being or just a native species of Earth.

So, while in Lemuria we had started communicating and wandering together, the first true communities were formed in Atlantis.

These Atlantean communities were developed by one of the angelic Orders called Hapiru. We could tell many long stories about Hapiru, but they were a very highly refined spiritual family. They tended to keep to themselves, so they connected with each other on Earth – Hapiru to Hapiru, physical body to physical body – and began to develop their own type of community. They wandered off to a different part of the landforms on Earth and set up their community, and one of their primary objectives was to standardize the biological body.

If you could imagine, back in Lemuria we had beings of all sizes and shapes, different brain structures and different cellular structures. But Hapiru, a very advanced angelic Order, began setting up a standardized template, which you now know as the human body. Back then it was much more apelike, as you have learned from your evolution courses, but there was deliberate work, both from a biological, scientific standpoint, and also from an energetic standpoint, to standardize the human bodies.

Over a period of time this development started attracting other souled beings, and spirits who were ready to reincarnate began coming to this land of Atlantis. We liked the idea of standardizing, and eventually this whole concept of a standardized human biological vessel is actually what caused Lemuria to become extinct. Who wanted to be a big old fat bird when you could have a body shape that looked like everybody else? Who wanted to be a dinosaur at a dinner party where everyone else looked like an ape? So there became a strong tendency or pull to incarnate in the lands of Atlantis.

The early work in Atlantis was all about standardizing the height and shape of the human body, the bone structure, the organs, and all of what you now know as the medical or scientific aspects. It was done in a variety of ways, often through very careful pairing of masculine and feminine bodies with certain attributes. Sometimes it was done energetically, using crystals and the crystalline energies of Earth to really focus on some of these developing human attributes. Some of the work was done surgically, and some of it was done using very strong "magnetic" energies, although different than the magnetics that you have now. Over much time, as this work went on, the human body did indeed become quite standardized.

The next step was to begin standardizing the mind. Even with the developing human biology, we still had different mental capabilities and different sizes of the brain. But we all wanted to have about the same size head, so we began the work of developing the human mind.

This was truly an amazing time. We were now very deep into the human process and were beginning to take ownership of our body and mind. And we had completely forgotten our origins, who we were and where we came from.

I have to point out here that in this time of Lemuria and Atlantis there was no concept of God. In Lemuria we were busy just being biological. In Atlantis we started looking for the Source, because we knew there must be a Prime Energy somewhere, but there was no concept of God like what humans have now.

At first, we thought this Prime Energy was in the Earth itself. We found crystals, and back then the crystals held amazing energies, far more than what they do now. Remember, the crystals were planted there by Gaia for the humans to use in making it easier to be in human form.

So, at first, we thought that the Source energies were the crystals. Well, they weren't, but we did find in them incredible types of energies that helped us to absolutely focus ourselves and get into a hypnotic state. And in this type of hypnotic state we were able to do incredible things like lifting objects without physically touching them and building what you now know as your pyramids, where even modern engineering is perplexed at how these were built. It was through some of these very beautiful and intense energies, coming from the crystals of Earth through our physical bodies in a very focused way, that we were able to do incredible feats.

So, we began to standardize the mind so that everybody had about the same size of brain with about the same capabilities. But, humans being as they are, there were some who wanted a little bit better body and a little bit bigger brain, and here is where a lot of the human imbalances started coming in.

Atlantean Wounds

The original family group of Hapiru, who founded Atlantis, took a certain ownership of it. They felt that they deserved more mind power, better crystals to work with, and more glamorous and attractive bodies. Obviously, this type of entitlement creates imbalance and, within the humans now, it created an imbalance that eventually led to the downfall of Atlantis.

It also eventually led to a very deep wound in the family group. Hapiru, who were extremely intelligent and very capable of focusing energy, saw nothing wrong with having slaves and controlling other humans. There was a time in Atlantis where Hapiru represented only about three percent of the total population, but they controlled the other 97 percent. They thought they were doing good, but did not realize there were some within their own family of Hapiru, and also some from other families, who had tapped into some of these powers and were using it against others.

Through the things that were done during this time of Atlantis, the family of Hapiru developed an incredible group karma and, unfortunately, many of them are still suffering for it today. Many of them, at the soul level, still will not let themselves forget the times of Atlantis and the imbalances that were created. You know Hapiru now as the Jews, which I, and likely you, have been also.

They have always been a type of family, and even to this day they have many of their own ways. They intuitively understand that they come from a special spiritual family, perhaps no more special than any other, but they're still carrying much of this group karma with them, and they still allow themselves to continually suffer.

By the way, Hapiru is more than just what you know today as the Jews. The Hapiru family encompasses the Palestinians and many others in the area of the Middle East, many of whom are also still carrying some of the old Atlantean karma. It is my sincere wish, having spent much time with Hapiru, that they can release this old karma and that those who are enlightened spiritual beings will release them from the karma as well. There is no need to suffer anymore. Humanity doesn't need another Holocaust.

Back to Atlantis

So much work had been done to conform the bodies, which were very standardized now, making it much easier to practice medicine, to fit for clothing, and to pair with other humans. And the search for the Source of life went on. We had found that it wasn't in the crystals, so we thought perhaps it was in the sky, in the stars. Again, there was no concept or word for "God." We were just trying to find Source, trying to find out where energy came from, where it was being made, and how we could get more. And this is another important point.

As far back as I can remember the world has had an energy crisis, because there are always some who believe in lack and want more. There is no lack of energy at all. It is abundant. There is more than enough for everyone. You don't need to hoard energy in terms of dollars, food, psychic ability or anything else. You just need to know how to efficiently use what you already have. You could have just a tiny particle of pure energy and it would be enough to sustain you for a hundred lifetimes, but there is this belief that energy is scarce, that you have to grab your share and consume as much as you possibly can. It is not so at all.

Eventually, not finding this Source in the stars or the outer realms, we began to suspect that it was inside the human body. So, we started doing a lot of experiments, cutting people apart – yes, even before they were dead – trying to find this Source. Of course, first we tried the dead ones, but not finding the Source there, we tried it on the ones who were alive, thinking that it still remained within them. Of course, we still didn't find it, but we did gain a tremendous amount of knowledge about biology, and we learned how to refine the physical body and the mind even more.

To assist with the mental refinements and standardization, there were many, many who wore a type of metal headband. It was used as a way of helping to tune the mental frequencies. Many humans still symbolically wear these headbands, trying to become really smart, trying to increase their mental capability. And this is fine as long as it is balanced with the spirit and the body.

Perhaps you can already guess the next part of the story. These headbands and mental manipulations led to mind control, which led to yet a further separation between our spirit, our body and our mind. The mind now became king.

Who was smarter? Who was more cunning? Who could best use the mind to focus energy while forgetting about the body and the spirit? Who could control? And once again, we got back into our games of stealing energy from others and trying to attain power. We weren't necessarily doing it now by trying to devour another person, although there were some back in Atlantis who practiced that. Now it was done in different ways. There were those who used the mind and mind control to steal from others, and this led to great battles in the end days of Atlantis.

The Downfall of Atlantis

In the end days of Atlantis there was a warrior by the name of Azuru Timu. He was called the Blue One or the Blue Ghost because his skin had a very blue cast to it, and he tried to amass as much power as possible. He used these metal headbands for mind control, manipulation and hypnosis, and any time there is an imbalance like this, it leads to conflicts and wars.

We hadn't seen wars in a long, long time, since long before coming to Earth, and unfortunately, they were back. But remember, a very important reason for coming to Earth was to relive experiences that we had had in the angelic realms. And now we were finally bringing them to Earth, recreating them in a very physical way so that we could gain wisdom and understanding from the experience. So, in a way, the energy feeding, the wars and the manipulation were inevitable and even necessary.

Unfortunately, there were other things that those who were hungry for power learned to use and work with, things like rape and torture. It's one thing to kill another being; they'll just come back in for another lifetime. But when you torture a human, it traps their spirit, putting it in such a wounded, traumatized state, that you can, for a period of time, manipulate it and use it to derive power and energy.

Rape is perhaps one of the most sadistic of all of the energies, one of the most heinous. When you rape someone, brutally and violently, you're taking a part of them. You are enslaving them, at least for a period of time, taking not just their body but part of their spirit and part of their mind. Unfortunately, these things started to become commonplace in Atlantis, contributing even more to the energy imbalances that led to the downfall.

The wars and abuse that took place also led to energetic imbalances in Earth itself, and these imbalances caused the weather patterns to change. There came violent storms, clouds developed that had never before been seen on Earth. Back in the days of Lemuria we had clouds that were very different than what you have now. They were very short and wouldn't block the sun like they do now. Now you have clouds that cover entire continents at a time, and weather patterns that are much more unstable than in the early days of Lemuria.

So, we had violent, violent storms in these last days of Atlantis. We had earthquakes, hurricanes, lightning storms that would last for months at a time, thunderstorms that seemed to settle upon certain conflicted regions of the land and basically annihilate entire populations.

There was such devastation that many of the humans who died in these end days of Atlantis went off into the Near Earth realms and hid.

They went into the quiet back spaces and hid away because they were so appalled at what was happening on Earth and so ashamed of being a human. They did not reincarnate for a long, long time, because Earth had become too violent.

Darkness

In the end days of Atlantis, there were small tribes or groups of humans who set off to try to find some new and calmer lands. Most of them didn't make it. Some of them did, but they were nomads, constantly traveling from one location to the other. They devolved, reverting back to some of the earlier animal-like features of the human body, going back to an ape-like form, because they were losing some of that energetic essence.

At this point animals began to fight with and eat other animals, because energetically they felt how humans were doing it to other humans. Species turned on species, parents turned on children, and everything went into destruction.

It was a dark, dark time for humanity, and you could say that humanity and even the animal kingdom was almost wiped from the face of Earth itself.

Sadness spread, not just throughout Earth and the Near Earth realms, but all the way back to your spiritual families, because they could feel that what had seemed to be the most promising of all the plans was not working. Sadness spread all the way back to the Wall of Fire.

Yet, back at Home in the kingdom of I Am, the heart of Mother-Father God continued to have hope and promise for this journey that you were on. They knew you were going through some of the darkest of times, they knew that the energies of failure and disappointment had overcome all humans, but they still had hope. They still knew you and they still loved you.

At this time there were some humans who understood that the surface of Earth was becoming far too violent with its storms and wars and fires everywhere, and it was here that groups of humans started to go underground. Some underground structures had already been built for a variety of purposes during the times of Atlantis, and many new ones now started to be built. They were built in conjunction with existing caves and openings into the Earth, and the humans started to migrate, over many thousands of years, going deep, deep into the Earth.

On the surface of the Earth all life seemed to burn and be destroyed and demolished. Beneath the surface of Earth, the humans who survived went deep within themselves.

And so it was, that darkness settled upon the Earth.

NOTES

NOTES

CHAPTER 9

OUT OF DARKNESS

And so it was, that all things on Earth and in the Near Earth realms went quiet. Small nomadic groups of humans wandered on the surface of the Earth, essentially with the sole purpose of preserving the human race.

Turning Inward

Simply struggling to survive, and in many ways reverting back to more primitive forms, they were unaware that beneath the surface were millions of human beings who had gone to take refuge deep within the Earth itself. And, in the Near Earth realms, those who had died as humans tucked themselves away in a type of spiritual hibernation, not preparing to come back to Earth for a long, long time. All things went quiet. All beings went deep within.

The ones who lived beneath the surface of the Earth relied on the crystals and the crystalline energies, planted there long before by Gaia, for light, energy, and even to help produce oxygen. They began to look deep within. They began to tell stories of Atlantis to their offspring, and to their offspring. They talked about the wonders of Lemuria and imagined someday recreating a society on the surface of the Earth when things had finally calmed down.

The ones who were hidden away in the Near Earth realms also took a deep, contemplative look at what had happened in Lemuria and Atlantis, and realized that so much more good than harm had taken place. Spirit, angels taking the form of humans, had been like children, playing wildly in the playground of Earth, forgetting to take responsibility for themselves, forgetting to be themselves, for indeed,

Atlantis had become so communal they had forgotten about the individual. Everything was done for the community good, but nothing for the individual. Scared to be alone or by themselves, everything had to be done as a group.

So we went through this very long, dark, quiet but peaceful period, looking within and beginning to heal the wounds that we had taken on in Lemuria and Atlantis. And, in the small tribes on the surface of the Earth, in the groups beneath the surface, and in those who were in the Near Earth realms, we began to take another look and another feel into that age-old question, "Who am I?" Examining that question brought about the contemplation of Spirit and the nature of reality. It caused another look into why we were here and what life was all about.

The Future is the Past Healed

On the surface of the Earth there were some, in the small groups of wandering humans, who intuitively knew that someday humanity would reemerge in a new and different and healed way. So they went off in small groups of their own to hold and to prepare the energies for those who would return. They did meditations and chants, and kept themselves in a type of trance state, maintaining a connection to the spiritual families and to the other realms.

Even today, these small groups continue to exist. Oh, they have gone through their own birth and death cycles, but these small groups, strategically located around the world, hidden to almost all other humans, exist to this day, continuing to hold the dream and the vision of the New Earth that is coming.

Approximately 25,000 years ago, those who had been beneath the surface of the Earth began to reemerge. They saw that nature was very resilient. They saw that Gaia had cleansed herself, the fires had stopped, the violent storms had balanced out, the forests were plentiful again with animals and insects, and the skies were filled with birds. Indeed, those who ventured to the surface realized that nature can handle herself, cleanse herself and rebalance herself.

They realized also that humans are resilient. They can go through some of the greatest challenges – mentally, physically, and even spiritually – and still they can heal their wounds. And this provided great hope for indeed it is known that the future is the past healed. What that means, dear friend, is the realization that all these experiences in the angelic and human realms have helped us all to grow, to realize who we truly are, and to begin understanding the answer to that original question, "Who am I?" With this understanding, the wounds of the past become healed, transmuted into wisdom.

When we look at the past from beyond the perspective of sadness and error, without judgment, without right or wrong, understanding it was part of our chosen experience, then the past is healed. And by healing, I mean that it is seen with wisdom and insight rather than judgment and scorn.

When we heal the past, when we accept it for what it was and all that it gave us, it changes the course of our future. For humanity, the future is generally determined by the past. The road of yesterday becomes the road for tomorrow, until the enlightened human stops for a moment and heals what came before by accepting it and embracing the wisdom. Then the path for tomorrow is changed.

I invite those who think humanity is headed down a wrong path right now to stop for a moment and realize that by accepting and healing the past, tomorrow will be different, because it is no longer the path of karma or destiny. Instead, it becomes the path of choice, imagination and creativity.

For those who think that the world is going to destroy itself soon, stop for a moment. It doesn't have to be that way, and actually, it won't be that way. But stop in your own life path for a moment. Take a look at the energies of all the time since you left Home, when you were in the angelic realms, going through the Order of the Arc, coming to Earth, your experiences in Lemuria and Atlantis, even your experiences in this lifetime.

Stop for a moment. Heal the past. Accept the experiences without judgment, without saying they were right or wrong. It was that it was. It was part of your growth, your insight and your learning. Accept the wisdom you have gained.

When you heal the past and then turn around and face your future, it changes all of that which was destiny, which had been created from the karma of your past. It changes the path that you were on, miraculously transforming it into new potentials that you couldn't have seen before. They were always there, but you could never see them through the lens of a wounded past.

Stop for a moment, in this precious Now moment. Take a deep breath, and accept everything about yourself, everything about the human journey, everything about those around you. Let go of judgments and opinions and the need to determine whether somebody was right or wrong.

Stop for a moment. No matter what happened, it was that it was. It was an experience that was chosen, for some divine purpose, by all of those involved.

Once you accept that, the road leading into your future changes. No longer does it have to be filled with struggles and obstacles and potholes. No longer does it have to be cruel and punishing, because when the past is healed, when the past is accepted, when the past is embraced, the road leading into the future is totally changed. It is now created by your choice in the moment.

A Consciousness of God

So, around 25,000 years ago, humans started to emerge from underneath. They came to the surface of the Earth with a different type of consciousness, with an understanding that there was something called Spirit, even though they didn't know how to define it. In Atlantis and Lemuria there was no concept of this thing called God. It was simply the search for the source of energy. But now, emerging onto the face of the Earth, was a new and different connection with Spirit.

Then, about 10,000 years ago, humans began to come up from within the Earth in larger numbers. And as they emerged with their new understanding of this thing called God, they began using the term "god" to understand or to justify things in nature and in the cosmos. They assigned a value of "god" to nature, which is actually very true, for there is a god of nature. They assigned a god to the sun, and indeed there is a spirit energy of the sun itself. Although it is not a souled being, the sun has its own identity and personality, its own consciousness of itself as the sun.

The ones who emerged from the Earth started assigning god values to everything around them, and in a way, they were very, very correct in this. But the one thing they were still missing was the understanding that they too were God, but a God of a different being, a God of a soul consciousness.

For a long period of time, gods were the hot item with humans on Earth. They assigned god values to little statues, to trees, to animals, to spirits, to everything they possibly could. Humanity went god-crazy, worshiping just about every type of god or image that came along, and for consciousness this was good. It helped create the understanding that we are much more than just humans, that other spiritual forces abound.

Eventually the emerging consciousness brought about the being you know as Abraham. Abraham had a difficult time keeping track of all these gods. There were tens, hundreds, thousands of different gods, and Abraham found this very confusing. His own father was a merchant of god paraphernalia, a god promoter, setting up a little stand that had statues and images of every possible god you could imagine, and selling them to the somewhat naïve residents of the community to handle every problem and issue that came up.

So, Abraham, who was actually a collective energy, said, "Let there be one God." Now, he got very close to the true understanding, but was still a little off, because he said the one God is out there somewhere, far away in heaven. He looked out to the stars and said, "That's where God must be." He was actually very, very close. If he had only brought it in a little bit closer and said, "I am God, just as you are God," he would have been truly accurate. But for now, it was close enough.

This change in the understanding of God ultimately created the religions that are predominant on Earth right now, the "one God" religions, and it spread very, very quickly. One human would whisper to another, "There is just one God now. All the rest have been wiped out." In a way, this was somewhat unfortunate because the whole Pagan understanding that God is in everythingwas also wiped out. There is a god-type energy or essence in the Earth and in the stars. There is indeed a spirit of the seas or the oceans. There is a spirit of the forests. They are not souled beings, but they have a consciousness, and they are here to serve you, the true God.

The Christos Era

Approximately 2,000 years ago the consciousness of Earth evolved and grew once again, and this created another collective being who came to Earth, the one that you call Yeshua, or Jesus. Yeshua was not a souled being. He was the manifestation of the consciousness of a group of humans who understood that the time was right; who understood that the divine energies of each and every angel on Earth would soon be coming to join that human, and that this would be a completion of a long, long cycle of experience and discovery.

When Yeshua came to Earth, there were tens of thousands of humans who also came to Earth at the same time, helping to support the Christos or the Christ Seed energy on Earth. Perhaps as you read this, dear child of Christ, you might remember that time when you came to Earth 2,000 years ago. Perhaps you didn't make the headlines like Yeshua did, but you also didn't have to end up on the cross. You came here to bring in some of the divine energies, to begin planting the seeds that would sprout 2,000 years later.

You began to open a type of spiritual or energetic corridor that would eventually be the pathway for your own divine essence to join you here on Earth. You weren't trying to change other humans, you weren't trying to start churches, and you weren't trying to start a movement. You were quietly doing your own work. You may have been one of the meditators and energy holders who were in these small groups during this long, long time span between Atlantis and the Christos era. Perhaps you had sequestered yourself in the Near Earth realms, staying away from all of the other entities and even from Spirit, breathing in a spiritual and energetic way, imagining the new Earth.

Imagination

I'm going to stop here for a moment and talk about imagination. Imagination comes from the heart. Imagination is bringing in, feeling and embodying the energies of the potentials that you are choosing. All around you are the myriad of potentials of everything that could ever be in your future. Imagining from your heart the potential that you're choosing brings that potential to the forefront and makes it more likely to become manifest on Earth than all of the other potentials.

When you open your imagination, when you stop denying it and pushing it down, it creates real energy movement that can eventually bring in potentials from the other realms to become very tangible and real here on Earth. When you allow yourself to imagine and to breathe with that imagination, it opens up something within you and within the safe space around you to help make that potential a true reality.

So those who came in at the time of Yeshua had been imagining the world that could be. They had been imagining the energies of all of the cosmos freeing up, opening up and moving again. They imagined something that we now call New Energy, because although they had no mental idea of what it was like, they could imagine its grandness.

Two thousand years ago so many who are here right now – and you who are reading this – imagined the potentials. You came to Earth and incarnated, not just in the lands of Israel and the Middle East, but all around the world. You incarnated in India, Africa, South America, Asia – all over the world – to bring in the seeds of Christ consciousness. And it truly changed the world.

Continuing the Christos Era

Look at it today. See the effect that it had, not just in the religions that were built since then, but the effect of consciousness on Earth. Yes, you've gone through difficult and challenging lifetimes since then, but beautiful lifetimes as well. In fact, it's interesting to note that, after the lifetime in the time of Yeshua, so many then came in for lifetimes as rabbis, priests and nuns. Many went into the convents and the monasteries, continuing to imagine and breathe in that energy.

At last, after many lifetimes on your hands and knees, after many lifetimes of ceremony and religious rhetoric, you got very, very tired of the religions. You saw what was happening, how the mind was taking over, how the religions were losing their hearts, becoming very dogmatic and rote, filled with human rules rather than God's rules. If you look back to the early days of the Christian church, they knew the mysteries. They understood many of the basic connections with Spirit, and one thing they truly understood were the words that were spoken from Yeshua's mouth:

"The Kingdom that is within me is a Kingdom that is within you."

"In my house there are many mansions."

"You are God also."

But, even though you had had enough of the religions, you also knew the time wasn't quite right for humanity to awaken. It might have been right for you, but it wasn't yet quite right for humanity. Human consciousness was still emerging and maturing and evolving, still going through its gyrations, so you patiently waited.

You left the churches and often, when you came back in the next lifetime, you were quite a loner. You stayed away from groups and definitely stayed away from the religions. Perhaps you went into the secret Mystery Schools of Adamus Saint-Germain. Perhaps you simply led a very quiet, simple life, allowing yourself a bit of rest and quiet space, just enjoying life on Earth. But all the time knowing deep within you that this time of the New Energy era was drawing near.

This Lifetime

Eventually, you chose to incarnate again, probably soon after World War II, knowing that it had the potential to be the grandest time of change on Earth ever – grander than Lemuria, grander than Atlantis or even the Christos era. You also knew that it had the potential for destruction, depending on which way human consciousness chose to go.

So you came to Earth, perhaps incarnating into a biological family that you had never been with before, or perhaps incarnating into a biological family that you had karmic ties with but, if you had been perhaps in a better state of spirit, you wouldn't have chosen them at all. But they were there, they were available, so you grabbed the body and came in.

You also brought with you a lot of the anxiety from Atlantis, because you knew it was another turning point on Earth. You knew that in the year 1999 there would be the final decision: Would we go through another version of Atlantis, perhaps with a nuclear war, perhaps with some type of storms or climate change that would bring another destruction to Earth? Destruction, by the way, is usually just a cleansing process, clearing out old energies to make way for the new. But you also knew there was the potential for humanity to continue beyond 1999.

Now, it wasn't just that 1999 was the last year of the millennium. It was also a marker, an end of the old era and a potential beginning of the new, and perhaps you felt uncertainty and anxiety. Oh, you busied yourself with your day-to-day work, perhaps raising a family, having a job and a career, but all this time, well, let's say that you knew you were a bit different. You knew that you had chosen to be here for a very special reason.

You tried to blend in, you tried to be normal, but it just didn't work. And you really struggled with it. You had dreams that told you there was something different. It wasn't that you were better than others, you just had a little bit different vision than most.

When you were very, very young, you spoke with the angels. You talked with the nature devas and fairies. You had friends that weren't in physical body that you talked to all the time, and this was all very natural for you. It seemed very unnatural that others around you didn't do these things. Perhaps you could move objects without touching them, simply by being within them, because you remembered the days when you allowed yourself to be in a tree or an animal and to move and shape and shift its energies. Perhaps you could read the minds of other humans very easily, because you were taught to do this in Atlantis. Perhaps you also knew very well how to travel without leaving your body, to do what we call remote viewing, to go into the past or into the future and feel into the potentials. All of this is natural for you. It is part of who you are.

You came into this lifetime so excited and exuberant because you knew there was a great potential for this to be *the* time on Earth. You were so enthusiastic and filled with energy, and you just burst onto the scene. Whether your parents were expecting a child or not they got one, because you helped facilitate that. Don't ever look back on the past or on your parents in a disparaging way; it was a way for you to come in, to be here now.

But, even then, the energies still weren't quite ready. You thought you were going to get this grand reception by the humans around you, welcoming you in as this wise being. But instead, you saw them giving you that look, making you feel ashamed, telling you that you were making it up. Ah, I think that's one of the most difficult wounds, being told that you were just "making it up." You weren't making it up; it was real, but they kept on enforcing that. Perhaps you received physical abuse. Almost certainly you received a lot of mental abuse, hearing things like "What's wrong with you? Can't you be like the others?

Why are you so quiet? Why do you just talk to yourself? You have to study" – ah, back in the mind here – "You have to be a good student. You have to follow the rules."

The interesting thing was, because you wanted to please and because you have such a love for humanity, you allowed yourself to shut down, albeit reluctantly and painfully. In fact, you didn't just shut down. You actually took your energy and twisted and warped it. You tried to burn away some of that energy, literally and figuratively, tried to lock it away, to do anything so that it wasn't real anymore. In doing so, you also did some damage to your physical body. You hurt yourself as part of this process of shutting down, for it was also hurting yourself for your humanness. Some of this pain of closing down is still showing up in your body today. What had been a most beautiful thing turned into yet another tragedy for you, and you shut down for a long time.

Eventually you started questioning, wondering at a deeper level, asking yourself "Why am I here? What's the purpose? What's the meaning?" You started to question the purpose of life, and unfortunately, because you were suppressing your own energy, it started to cause depression. That's what happens when you suppress the natural flow of energy.

So you started going to others for advice – "What's wrong with me?" – and they would give you their human interpretation, not at all understanding your spirit. Then you really felt lost and sad and alone. You tried to stay normal – for your children, for your spouse, for the people you worked with – but it wasn't working very well.

Then along came these little drugs that they have now, mind altering, mind suppressing drugs that actually trigger you back to these times of Atlantis with the headbands. And, because they cause even further separation within you, that created even deeper depression. You began wonder, "Do I even want to be here?" You knew it wasn't suicidal. You weren't trying to make other people feel bad or trying to get even with others by some dramatic act of suicide. You just wondered, "Should I really be here? What's it all about?" And just that very consciousness, the lack of truly breathing in life, starts to cause a death process.

Sometimes this whole act of hiding felt so difficult and painful that seemed easier to die, so you stopped breathing. In other words, you took in just barely enough air to survive rather than deeply breathing in life. You stopped being filled with passion. You stopped enjoying the beauty of nature and the love of other humans. You made yourself cynical so you didn't have to be present anymore, but you were missing something. You were missing the grandest change ever, the beauty of life, this amazing evolution. You were missing the New Energy.

A New Life

Then something happened to you, perhaps a year ago, five years ago, ten or twenty years ago. Suddenly something inside you snapped. It was a reminder that, fortunately, you had planted there a long time ago, a reminder that we call "the Fruit of the Rose." It was the reminder to your spirit, to your life, that you are here for a reason, that you are an angel, that there is a blessing, that life can be joyful, and you started searching.

You started reading, going to classes, searching online, and perhaps you finally found a group of humans who you have been with before. Maybe it was in Lemuria, where one of you looked like a big bird and the other looked like a lizard, but you remembered. And you remembered being together in Atlantis. And you especially remembered a time at the end of Atlantis when we were together in a place called Tien, in the temples, where we had just begun to understand the simple concept that God is within and that all you need to do is love yourself and you'll understand who you really are.

You remembered that you had known each other in the times of Yeshua, and now you are back, together on Earth again. Whether you even know of the Crimson Circle or what we call Shaumbra is irrelevant, because you are energetically connected. Some have connected very directly, face to face, and created this thing on Earth now called Crimson Circle. And you reminded each other, by looking in each other's eyes, of why you're here. You're here because it truly is the completion of the circle. It's about that inner knowingness, the feeling of "That's right! I *am* here for a reason and it's not about my job. It's not about my title, how much money I have, or even my family. I'm here because I chose it for me. I'm here because I wanted to be here to celebrate this thing called New Energy."

New Energy

So, what is New Energy? New Energy was the hope, the design, the final segment of the journey. New Energy is not vibrational or dualistic like the energy of Earth and all of creation currently is. It is expansional, expanding in every direction at once. It doesn't need to push against itself. It doesn't need the friction of vibrational energy to create reality. It is created and works in a whole different way. New Energy coexists with vibrational energy. It doesn't destroy it or over-come it, and eventually vibrational energy will adapt the conscious-ness of New Energy to itself.

Vibrational energy, the energy you're familiar with, has been around as long as you have been on this side of the Wall of Fire. Re-member we said that the volume or the quantity of energy has always been the same. You've just been transmuting it, changing it and put-ting it into different forms to create your experience on Earth. There has always been a finite number of souled beings on this side of the Wall of Fire, and those souled beings have been using the defined quantity of old energy to create reality and experience.

You could say that Spirit gave you a certain amount of energy and said, "Go play with it. See what you can create. See what you can de-stroy. Keep playing with the energy and see what you can experience." But now something new is happening. New Energy began coming in a few years ago, very subtly. It has never existed before. It wasn't in the original gift box that Spirit gave you. It's not from Spirit, not from Home, not from the Kingdom. It's brand new and this means something very important: Angels have created it.

Angels, humans, have created new energy for the first time ever. Simplifying that statement: You are now a creator. Instead of just taking something that always was, that was given to you by Spirit, and playing with it, reshaping it, re-forming it, now you have created, in your own right, literal New Energy.

It's going to take a long time for the scientists and technicians to understand what it is and how it works. New Energy is very elusive when measured against old vibrational energy. It's very difficult to analyze because it doesn't respond like old energy, and it's very difficult to quantify because it doesn't act like old energy.

Quantum physicists are beginning to see it, but not at all to understand it yet, so they call it chaos, because it doesn't react like they think it should. And it absolutely is chaos, because, in a way, in true physics everything is chaos, and it should be. Real energy is not in order until it is commanded into order, and eventually it has to be released out of that order for it to continue to expand.

So, here is the advent of New Energy. It's no longer a hope or a promise, it is absolutely real and making its way to Earth. Minute "particles" of it are already here, and those particles are going to be attracted to humans who have accepted everything about themselves, who are learning to love themselves, and who are open to exploration and expansion.

The very existence of New Energy says that the energy and consciousness in the other realms, back in your spiritual families, is finally going to begin moving and expanding. In fact, your spiritual families have rejoiced because they knew it, even before you did. They could sense it, and several years of your time ago the movement of all creation – not just your physical universe, but of the entire cosmos – started expanding again, slowly but very definitely.

That is to say, dear friend, that the plan of Earth worked.

No one is sure, exactly – if you were to measure it in human terms – how fast, but we know it's expanding. We know now that existence is not going to collapse on itself. We know that we have fulfilled what we came here to do – become creators in our own right – and there's no doubt about it.

And, back at Home, the metaphorical King and Queen – which are outdated terms as of right now – they know it also. Even though you were tied up with the dramas of this lifetime, they applauded and cheered because you did it. You created New Energy on your own, and it's going to continue expanding in every direction at once.

Obviously, it's going to cause a lot of changes on Earth, but the changes will come about in a very smooth and beautiful way, because that is what you have imagined. The changes are going to affect fuel energy on Earth. You've been using old fossil fuel, a very old symbolic fuel, and that will change. You can feel the expansion going on right now. Technology is working on new energy sources, looking at things like wind and sun, or certain types of water, but that's just the tip of the iceberg.

New Energy is coming. New healing modalities – the ability to heal the body without having to cut into it or put harsh and abrasive medicines into it – these are some of the results of New Energy.

The shake-ups in the financial and political systems will continue happening, because expanding consciousness brings changes. And sometimes the old energy institutions don't like the changes, so it creates some conflicts. But you know what? It's going to work. The old energy, when it gets tired of battling and fighting, is going to lie, weary and tired, and finally accept that New Energy is here.

The churches are going to experience radical changes as well, because humans are going to begin understanding that the Source is within, that it isn't some God off in heaven who is directing their life and their destiny. Humans will begin to embrace the concept that "I am God also. I am a souled being," and as they do, it opens the pathway for the divine to come in, for Home to come to you, for your pure and very simple essence to join you in this reality.

Don't make it complex. Don't analyze your divine. Don't assign to your God-self some overwhelming power or quotient over you. It is so very simple, and in its simplicity is its magic and its marvel. In its simplicity is its purity and its essence, and it is finally melding with your humanity. You'll go through some changes, of course, because some of the old systems and thoughts and beliefs and understandings are going to have to change and transform in the pure understanding that you are God also. But all that you have hoped for, dreamed of and imagined for Earth is finally coming to be.

Dear friend, what an incredible journey we have shared from Home to here. What an incredible time to be on Earth. Perhaps you don't fully understand it right now, but this is an incredible time of fulfillment.

Now, perhaps you say, "Tobias, the road has been so long and difficult. What's to say that it's not going to continue to be long and difficult?"

Well, you are, because it is your choice. It's your trust in yourself. It's your letting down the guard of this illusion of who you think you are. It is your surrender and stepping into everything that you really are, human and divine. It is allowing yourself to breathe, to be, to live, to enjoy, and that is exactly why I'm coming back – not to save the world or continue some wretched karma from the past, but to be here on Earth for the joy of life.

And so it is, that we have been on this journey together, that we have come to this miraculous time, that we are going through the grandest changes. Yes, these changes are sometimes difficult on the body, and they are definitely difficult on the mind.

Indeed, the mind is screaming out at times because it doesn't understand. It was so highly programmed in the times of Atlantis, and you still rely on it. But I want you stop and talk to your mind sometimes, rather than your mind talking to you. Acknowledge it and give it credit, and also let it know that it doesn't have to perform in the same way. It doesn't have to carry the burden and the responsibility anymore. It can be part of the fully integrated Self, but now the divine intelligence is going to be in charge, working with the mind but is no longer governed by it.

You're going to go beyond the mind, but you don't have to force this or study anything or do disciplines and ceremonies. You just have to be willing to allow this next step, the integration of the body, mind, spirit and divinity into this reality right here on Earth.

We've gone through the history of all creation in a very short period of time, but in a way you could say that it's taken us a hundred times longer to explain it than the time in which it actually happened. It is time now to let go of the concepts of time and space and go beyond, because that's why you're here right now, as a pioneer of consciousness.

What an incredible opportunity for us here to join our energies together to tell this story in a way that's understandable, where we don't get overly philosophical, where it goes straight to the heart. What a grand opportunity for I, Tobias, to tell the story to my next incarnation about how it got here.

And so it was.

NOTES

NOTES

CHAPTER 10

THE FUTURE IS THE PAST HEALED

And so it is, dear friend, that there is nothing more beautiful – or more challenging – than to be in physical form. I, Tobias, have spent hundreds and hundreds of lifetimes on Earth. I came in with so many of you in that first wave of angelic beings who came to Earth, coming through the tunnel or portal that compressed and compacted our energy, tightened up our consciousness and caused us to forget our angelic origins.

We all went through that experience, and what a grand experience it was. Many of us who came through this original portal to Earth found our way to what you now know as the lands of Hawaii, for that was the first, the original portal. Can you imagine the sense of beauty and majesty that we felt when we first arrived on Earth? This was created for us by Gaia, by the Order of the Arc, and it was going to be our playground for eons of time.

This Wonderful World
How amazing it was to allow ourselves to go so deep into experience that we ended up in physical reality, the densest and the most real of all of the dimensions. It allowed us to really take a look at ourselves, going through this very slowed-down energy, taking on different aspects and lifetimes, playing with energies in ways that the other angels cannot do.

Even to this day, the angelic beings who have never been to Earth are in such awe of those of us who have been here. They can't possibly imagine what it's like to be in a physical body, to touch another person, to eat food and take in nourishment. Well, perhaps they can imagine, because angels have wonderful imaginations, but only up to a point; and that point is actual experience. Nothing beats experience.

So we came in to this beautiful place, and back Home in All That Was, in the Kingdom, the hearts of the King and Queen have been swelling ever since. They don't get caught up in it when we go through our bad days or when we experience things like suffering and trauma and disease, because they understand that we are in experience. We're on a journey and we will come through it. It has always been known and it always is that we will come through it as sovereign beings. We will fulfill ourselves.

This whole thing with the slow-down of energy in the cosmos, this impasse, it wasn't a mistake at all. When the consciousness stopped expanding, when there was the concern from all of the angelic families, it was the wonderful opportunity to create this place called Earth. To come here and live within our own creation. To live within density and matter. It was a beautiful, beautiful creation, and it was not a mistake. It was done so we could be within our own Garden of Eden, with the freedom to do anything we wanted and express in any way we wanted, to be destructive and joyful, to steal energy from others and have ours stolen. But ultimately, it was to learn that it is all within, and it always has been.

Through all of this your spiritual families have stayed in contact with you. They get regular news reports on how you're doing, your trials and tribulations, and they have so much compassion for you. They understand your bravery. They understand how courageous you are and how difficult it is. They know that at times you feel so totally lost and alone and disconnected from your own origins, and they're constantly sending their love and cheering you on.

They can't do it for you. They can't create your reality for you, but they're cheering on the part of you that is the true creator; the part of you that can overcome the challenges and see through the darkest of times; the part of you that knows you're really not lost. You're in this grand experience called human life, and it will ultimately lead you to finding yourself in a whole new way, a way that could not have been done in the other realms. And it will also free their energy so they can continue to expand.

This thing we call your divine, the inward-looking Self that was placed in a cocoon such a long time ago, it has also been aware of everything – every thought, every feeling – and it transmutes everything. Even the darkest, most difficult experiences, what you call your bad thoughts and negative feelings – your divine transmutes those within itself into wisdom, beauty, and pure essence.

Your divinity is the simple, pure part of you that can never be damaged, destroyed or tarnished. It never has a judgment of you. It's always there, always part of you, and it never says, "You've taken a wrong turn" or "You're on the wrong path" or "Why is it taking you so many lifetimes to fulfill your journey?" It is just there, loving you, taking everything of this external expression and transmuting it into a depth of soul, into a light beyond light, into wisdom that is eternal.

What a grand experience we've all been having, filled with both the 'good' and the 'bad.' Oh, we've all had the darkest of moments and the most challenging of times, but we go beyond. We overcome. We learn from each experience.

None of these experiences are given to us as lessons from God. Please let go of that old, old concept. None of these are truly karma. In other words, our soul is not removed, sitting off someplace, making us go through these lessons to punish us or teach us like we were little children. The soul rejoices in every choice you make and every experience you have.

As one who has lived hundreds and hundreds of lifetimes on Earth, I know what it's like to lose connection with your roots, with your spiritual families, with some of these soul mates that you knew back in the earliest times after going through the Wall of Fire. I know what it's like to get so lost in the human experience you don't think you will ever get out.

To me, the most difficult of any of the challenges that we face as human angels, and one of the things that I'm the most passionate about, is the coming back to trust in ourselves.

The Shadow

When we left the Wall of Fire, part of our trust seemed to be taken away. We brought with us this thing called the Shadow, feeling that it was the dark and negative part of us. So, over eons of times and experiences and lifetimes, we have taken everything we don't love about ourselves and dumped it into the Shadow. We have cursed the Shadow and felt that it was our own demon, our own weakness. But it hasn't been.

The Shadow is the essence of us. It is the soul of us. It is the gift that Spirit gave to every one of us, in equal portions, that will never be taken away. It is us, our unique identity, the evidence that we exist, because any time a light falls on an object with it's own identity, it casts a shadow. So, as the light of Home falls upon our unique self, the Shadow reminds us that we are souled beings.

That Shadow we have cursed, that Shadow we have run from, that Shadow we have blamed for putting us into this endless cycle of lifetimes – that Shadow is our divinity, our soul. It is a reminder that Spirit has given us freedom and expression. Spirit loves us so much that Spirit said, "Go out and experience, without any judgment from me. Freely experience anything you want, because someday you will be a creator just like I am. You will be all that you are."

All these things like guilt and shame, things we despise and loathe about ourselves, we dump into this Shadow. It contains and holds it all, lovingly and without judgment. Sometimes we look at the Shadow and say, "How despicable it is. If I didn't have that Shadow, if I didn't have these dark parts of me, how perfect I would be." But the Shadow is our divinity.

It's the reminder that we came from Home. It's the part of ourselves that's going to love us, no matter what. You can choose any experience and that Shadow will be a reminder of the love. It's the divinity. It's the constant. It is always there.

The Loss of Trust

One of the most difficult things that we have felt, as we came into human form through this vast experience since leaving Home, was the loss of trust in ourselves. It was especially difficult when we came to Earth for the first time, went through the birthing process, and felt like we were stuck here in an endless cycle of lifetime after lifetime. We often repeated the same experiences over and over, expecting and hoping for a different outcome. And when that didn't happen, it caused us to lose trust in ourselves. And that loss of trust is perhaps the most painful and devastating thing an angel will ever experience, especially when we feel stuck here in biology and don't know the doorway to get out.

Humans don't know how to leave this planet. We try over and over to kill ourselves, subconsciously and sometimes consciously, thinking that the doorway out of this endless cycle of reincarnation lies in the graveyards of humanity. But it doesn't.

Imagine the sorrow and loss of trust a human has when, in despair and agony, they find a way to take their own life, hoping it is the key to escape this cycle of lifetimes, hoping to awaken from what appears to be a nightmare, and they get to the non-physical realms on the other side and find there is no key. What a loss of trust that causes, putting more distance between ourselves and our divinity, making us run even further from this thing we loathe and hate, called the Shadow.

Imagine, then, how it feels when the only alternative for this one who has lost hope and trust is to dive back down into yet another birth, feeling that they are totally out of control, being sucked back to Earth, back into their nightmare.

The loss of trust is the distance, measured in terms of consciousness, between ourselves and our own Spirit and divinity.

Loss of trust often begets more loss of trust and more running from ourselves, for when we loathe ourselves and forget to love ourselves, what do we do as human angels? We push our divinity even further away. We turn our back on ourselves, on Spirit, and on all things grand and glorious, because we don't think we deserve it. We literally set up entire lifetimes where we don't allow ourselves to enjoy the beauty of this planet and the experience of being human.

Falling In Love

There is no better place in all of creation, including the original Kingdom, where you can learn to love yourself like you can right here on Earth. There is no better place to fall in love with every part of you than right here, and that is the key to going beyond.

You're not going to do it when you release your physical body in death and go to the other side. Yes, you may rest and recuperate, but too many times humans go to the Near Earth realms in almost a nightmarish state. When you leave Earth, you don't go to some place called heaven. Most humans stay very connected to Earth when they die. They shed their physical body but carry just about everything else with them to the other realms. They don't go there and find some idyllic place to love themselves, just because they're free of their body. In fact, so often they are even more confused and traumatized than when they were here on Earth. Sometimes they come back to Earth as soon as they possibly can, trying once again to forget and escape themselves, to once again get lost in this density. So, when they come back to the other side and try to run from themselves, they just get into their minds.

The mind is such a perfect place to escape having to deal with the love of yourself. It is easy to occupy your mind with facts and figures and details and analysis so you can forget about actually loving you. You can build this false temple of the mind to pretend that you're smart and that you know things; but you're still running away, and you still know it.

So, we go through these endless cycles, one after the other, and the saddest thing is, when we do that we're forgetting to love the experience.

I, Tobias, am at the point in my evolution, in a way just like you are, where I don't need to come back anymore. I've gone through my series of lifetimes, and, using human terms, I went through my own ascension, which simply means I totally accepted myself. Spirit didn't grant me my 'ascension papers,' because Spirit already knew I was going to become whole unto myself. I didn't need the Order of the Arc to give me a certificate saying that I ascended.

Ascension occurred in the moment I surrendered to the love of my Self. It occurred in the moment when I said, "I Am that I Am, and I love everything about myself – without shame, without guilt, without reservation, without ifs, ands or buts." Ascension occurred when I surrendered into who I actually am, rather than to the aspects I had created trying to pretend I was something else. Ascension occurred when I knew within my heart that I am, I always was, and I always will be.

So, you may wonder why I have chosen to come back to Earth. It is not because the forces of karma have drawn me here, not because I'm trapped in a cycle of incarnations, but because there is no grander place than Earth, and all of the angels know it. In fact, of all of the 33 plans that were developed to expand consciousness, there is no grander one than this.

It is now known that all angels who are ready to once again absolutely trust themselves, who are ready to understand that all enlightenment and gifts are within if you simply allow yourself to unlock them, they will come by way of Earth. It is known that all of the angels of all of the cosmos and all of the dimensions, even all of those in your spiritual families, will eventually come by way of Earth in their ascension.

Now, they will come not only to just this physical Earth. This was the first of many, many Earths that are now being developed in your physical universe. What has been started here on Earth and everything we have come to learn – about life force energy, about biology and creating aspects of ourselves within biology, about the non-physical realms that surround this planet, about magnetic, electromagnetic and crystalline energies, about incarnations and suffering and redemption and all of these other things – these are all serving as a type of cosmic DNA that, at this very moment, is being breathed into other rocks around this physical universe in order to make room for other angelic beings who will come.

Earth – this human Earth you have right now – will always be the first. It will always be the template, the library for the other physical Earths. They will have different names, of course, and different types of attributes, depending on the angelic beings going there. But this, dear human, was the first, and you were among the first to come here. What an incredible journey it has been.

How to Trust?

Trusting in oneself is one of the most important and perhaps one of the most elusive things that a human will ever do. How do you trust yourself when you feel like you are trapped in biology? How do you trust yourself when you have done what you would consider to be very heinous deeds? How do you trust yourself when you feel the flesh is weak? How do you trust yourself when you don't even understand your own heart, your own emotions and your own feelings? How do you trust yourself when you feel powerless? How do you trust yourself when you're broke and don't have a dime? How do you trust yourself when you thought you finally understood your body, how its energies worked and how to sustain and support it, but it is once again giving out on you?

How do you trust yourself? Each moment without trust, each experience of limitation, causes another degree of separation between you and who you really are, between you and your Spirit, your essence, your divinity.

How do you trust your humanness to invite your divine here to Earth? Because that's what it takes. That is the ascension – when you can love yourself so much that you can invite the divinity, wrapped in its cocoon for its inward-looking experience, into this reality. It wants to be here with you. It's not resisting you, but you are not trusting yourself.

How many times have you given yourself excuses? "I'll move a little bit closer to my divine when I can manage or control some of my human weaknesses." "I have to lose weight first." Your divinity doesn't care how big or little you are. It loves you no matter what.

How many times have you withheld your own ascension because you want to get it right or perfect? You want to be smarter. You have to read more books and go to more workshops before you can invite your divinity in, because you think your divinity doesn't want a dumb human.

How many times do you say that you have to find peace within yourself first? How many times do you think that you have to kick your "bad" habits before you can invite your divinity to be with you?

So you play this game of stalling and delaying, but it's really just a lack of trust. Your divine, your essence doesn't care one bit about all those things.

The Love and Trust of Self

Your essence isn't going to come in and save you, and that's another delaying tactic. Sometimes you do beckon in your own divinity, but only to save you, only to rescue the humanness of you, only to give you a bit more power, which, by the way, is nothing but an illusion. Sometimes you want the divine to come in and repair or strengthen you, but then you're going to push it away again.

So, your I Am presence just waits patiently, allowing you to make that deep, true choice within, the choice that says "I am ready. No matter what, I am ready to integrate every part of me in total, absolute love, no ifs, ands or buts. I am ready to be who I am."

At that point another form of delay or reluctance comes in because you can sense very deep within that in this moment of pure, simple acceptance, of making that choice to absolutely trust yourself again, that your life will change. Are you afraid of those changes and what they might bring? Are you afraid that the moment you make that choice, you may die? Of course, it doesn't really matter, but your humanness screams out, "I don't want to die!" Well, I did, in my last lifetime, when I experienced my ascension. I'm not recommending that you do it the way I did, but I did and it didn't matter.

Do you consider making the choice to absolutely love and trust yourself, but then worry about what your kids might say? Will having absolute love and trust for yourself mean you'll lose your partner? Or your job?

Are you loading up your own boat with everyone else, thinking that you have to take them on the journey along with you? Do you think that the whole world of humans needs to ascend together? Where did that come from? That's a lack of compassion. There are beings here on Earth who have only been here a few times and have chosen what you would consider a very rudimentary and perhaps difficult path. There are other humans who have been here only a few lifetimes who understand some of the pure simple spiritual physics of being here, such as falling in love with yourself and then allowing yourself to ascend. Every human angel is at their own perfect point on the path.

Are you loading your own boat up with everyone else's problems and thinking that until you solve their problems and fix the Earth you can't ascend? In a way, you're desperately trying to cling onto those very things that are causing the lack of trust and the lack of love.

Dear one, this issue of trusting self is perhaps the biggest issue that you, as a very wise spiritual being, are facing. How do you trust who you are? As all of the aspects and voices come back and say, "Yes, but remember when you did this? Remember when you went wrong over here? Remember how you made a fool of yourself there?" they suppress the trust.

Trust is the total acceptance and knowingness – not in the brain, but in the heart – that you are Spirit. Trust is understanding that you've already arrived at your ascension. You're already there. You don't need to plan and plot. You don't need to make deals with Spirit. You don't need to follow certain rituals and go through specific ceremonies. It doesn't matter if you do yoga or eat cheeseburgers every day. It truly doesn't. Trust is knowing that you've already created your perfection. Now, can you live within it rather than hold it out somewhere else, far away?

Your state of what you would call perfection – divine balance, masculine-feminine integration, divine-human integration – it already exists. It's already created, but you keep it somewhere else. You're saving it, like you would put a bottle of fine wine in the back of your pantry, saving it for a special day. Why not pull it out right now? Why not be so in love with yourself today, understanding that changes will happen, but also understanding that you've already planned it, you've already created your divine life?

The Ascended Life

There's one more consideration here, because some people think that when you reach this state of ascension, which means absolute love of self, that you're going to vanish from the face of the Earth. And yes, it used to be that way. There are over 9,000 Ascended Masters who have gone through the trials and tribulations of lifetimes on Earth and have gone on to what we call their Third Circle or their state of sovereign divine existence. And generally, they would not come back to Earth. They would walk out, not to return.

But something very interesting is happening right now. We are starting to come back. The Ascended Masters are starting to come back, not to save the Earth but to experience the New Earth and the New Energy, right along beside you. We're not coming back to be your gurus or your masters; we're coming back to remind you that you are already your own master. We're coming back to remind you of the absolute joy of life, of being here on Earth. We're coming back to remind you that what Gaia created for you now becomes your own. We're here to remind you that there is so much beauty in life.

Being able to love yourself in physical form – there is nothing like it. Being able to love another human, take a walk in the woods, eat a meal, celebrate life with other humans without holding back – there is nothing else like it in all of creation.

I am coming back, dear friend, to join you. And I hope, as you absolutely fall in love with yourself, that you do plan to stay here on Earth for a while. You don't have to suddenly vanish, disappear, or go through the final death into the other realms, because there's a new type of birthing taking place right now. It is called mastery within the physical body, allowing this integration to happen. And yes, it's going to turn your life inside out and upside down for a short period of time. It may even bring about your final spiritual crisis while you are in human form, which for some of you is a most challenging experience. But it's part of the process of the transmutation of energy, of truly becoming all that you are.

If you just keep breathing and loving yourself, even when you're going through this difficult process, if you keep embracing whatever should happen to you, you'll find that you can stay right here on Earth in physical body, without having to die in your ascension, and you can enjoy life like you've always imagined. You can enjoy every experience, every lifetime you've ever had, without remorse or regret. I don't care what you did – it doesn't matter.

You can stay right here on Earth and choose, not out of fear, but out of love, to live to be 150 or 200 years old. And it is absolutely possible, if you love yourself.

I'm not talking about pretending to love yourself. I'm not talking about just the words, "I really love myself." I'm talking about falling in love with you. You know what it's like now to fall and be shattered and go through tunnels. You've done it. You've gone through the worst. So, what is it like now to fall in love with you?

Oh yes, every voice from your past, the voices of the aspects who are not yet integrated, they're all going to come out the moment you say, "I'm falling in love with me," because they've heard it before. A little bit different version perhaps, but they've heard it, and they're going to say, "Oh, here she goes again, here he goes again, another program, another method, another system, and we're going to use this to mock you even more, you silly, silly human."

But what if – just what if – you were so bold and courageous and outrageous that you let yourself fall in love with you without worrying about the consequences, without trying to control it or manage it, without trying to determine what it's supposed to look like? What if you just fell into the love of yourself and allowed it to be?

It will absolutely push your buttons and bring up your fears. It will absolutely cause some anxiety, so what do you do? You just take a deep breath and allow yourself to fully experience it instead of resisting, like we did going through the Wall of Fire. We resisted the love and the gift of Spirit, and that's what created the illusion of shattering. We resisted coming through this tunnel to Earth, even though we had chosen to do it, and that's what caused the feelings of compression and pain. But what if you, Master, fell in love with yourself and allowed yourself to hear and feel every voice, every fear, every potential and every emotion instead of resisting? What if, instead of running, you allowed yourself to connect back to your Shadow, your divine, and to be here on Earth as a fully conscious, trusting and aware angel?

Perhaps this is how you wrote out your own story of your lifetimes on Earth. Perhaps this is how you wrote out this chapter called "My New Energy." Perhaps you wrote it that you would live enough lifetimes right here on Earth to be here for the greatest change that Earth has ever seen, the greatest change in consciousness ever experienced, and the actual integration of New Energy. Perhaps you wrote it that you were here to experience it, to be part of creating it and then to stay here to work with it in absolute trust of self.

You cannot go wrong. You can pretend and have the illusion that you're going wrong, and you might be an absolute expert at playing the game of going wrong. You might even be so good at it that you continue to repeat that performance lifetime after lifetime. But what if this last chapter in your journey on Earth was the chapter when you said, "I'm going to be here at the beginning of the era of New Energy.

I'm going to be a pioneer once again, learning how to work with New Energy when most humans haven't a clue what it is, learning how to go beyond vibrational into expansional while here in the physical body experiencing it in the most intimate way. I'm going to fall madly in love with myself."

That's what life as a human is about – becoming truly intimate with yourself. That's why the Order of the Arc and all of the wisdom of all of the angels created Earth – for the intimacy with yourself.

What if, dear one, just what if you were among the first to stay here on Earth while absolutely loving yourself?

And so it is.

NOTES

NOTES

About Tobias

History: The Angel we know as Tobias lived many, many lifetimes on Earth. He takes his name from an apocryphal book of the Bible that records his lifetime as Tobit, an upright Jew in the lands of the Middle East. After being blinded in an unfortunate accident, Tobit's son Tobias embarked on a journey to help take care of the family business. His subsequent adventure, complete with a pet dog, a giant fish and an angelic traveler in disguise, has inspired countless retellings in stories and paintings.

After miraculously regaining his eyesight, Tobit lived many more years before he died and eventually returned for one final lifetime. Once again he lived as a righteous Jew in the land of Israel, but this time his fortunes turned sour. Betrayed and imprisoned, his land and family stolen, Agos, as he was then known, languished in despair for many years. Ill and nearing the end of his days, an angel appeared to him in the form of a bird, singing at the window of his prison cell of wonders far beyond. Agos let go of his anger and hate, and surrendered to the greatest love he would ever know, that of his own soul. Releasing the physical limitations, he experienced true enlightenment, left his physical body behind and assumed his place in the angelic realms as a fully ascended Master.

Current Era: In 1999 Tobias, assisted by Gabriel, Metatron and many others, sent out the clarion call of awakening and reunion. His monthly messages, channeled through his beloved former son, now known as Geoffrey Hoppe, quickly found their way to the hearts of awakening humans, those whom he had worked together with in times long past. With his messages of love, comfort and freedom, Tobias offered unceasing support for humans in what he called "the biggest evolution of consciousness humanity has ever experienced."

Tobias spoke through Geoffrey for ten years, and then chose to return to Earth for a long-awaited lifetime of celebration and joy. After years of preparation, Tobias gave his final message to humanity, released his angelic duties and fully entered his ten-year-old "shell" body on July 19, 2009. As he grows into a young man, we hope that one day Tobias will find his way back to the Crimson Circle and the beloved human angels with whom he has shared so much.

About Geoffrey & Linda Hoppe

Geoffrey Hoppe: The early spiritual curiosity of a young man was all but forgotten as he served a few years in the US Army as a Public Information Specialist at the NASA Ames Research Center (Mountain View, California), and then stepped into the business world. After finding his way to senior management positions in several advertising agencies, Geoffrey started his own marketing company in Dallas, Texas at the ripe old age of 28. Later on, he co-founded an aviation telecommunications company (provider of Internet services for business jets and commercial airlines, now known as Gogo), serving as Vice President of Sales and Marketing until 2001. In a stroke of ironic prescience, Geoffrey holds three patents for multidimensional telecommunications technologies, as well as numerous trademarks and copyrights.

Linda Hoppe: A gifted artist and highly creative by nature, Linda graduated Summa Cum Laude and went on to teach Art Education, even writing a ground-breaking curriculum for Texas' first high school honors Art Education program. Her artistic talents landed her a job as Fashion Merchandise Manager with a Fortune 500 company, helping to set the styles and designs for each upcoming season. She also served as manager for Geoffrey's marketing consulting company for several years.

Destiny: Geoffrey & Linda met in high school and got married in 1977 on the day the first Star Wars movie premiered. Twenty years later, an angel named Tobias introduced himself to Geoffrey during an airplane flight. After talking and learning together for an entire year, Geoffrey finally told Linda about his invisible friend. Soon after, Tobias started working with clients of a local psychologist, providing deep insights into past lives and current challenges.

In late summer 1999, a few friends were invited to listen as Tobias spoke through Geoffrey, assisted by Linda. It was the beginning of the Crimson Circle, an organization that they would soon spend every waking moment trying to keep up with. Since then, Crimson Circle has grown into a multinational organization, with Geoffrey & Linda traveling the globe conducting numerous workshops and events each year.

They didn't see it coming, but looking back in hindsight, they wouldn't change a thing in this most extraordinary lifetime.

About the Crimson Circle

I've often been asked, "What is the Crimson Circle?" Words escape me. My tongue gets twisted and my brain starts to spin. How can I describe something so deep – yet simple – and something so outside the realm of normal human thinking? How can I share the thousands of stories about humans around the world coming into their embodied enlightenment, and what the heck is embodied enlightenment anyway?

I used to launch into a long explanation, oftentimes losing my listener when I tried to explain the quest for truth, the wisdom of the Ascended Masters, our *real* purpose for being here on Earth at this time, the dynamics of channeling, the difference between consciousness and energy... well, you get the point. I got way too mental.

Now I just say, "You know what it's like... when you know there's more to life, but you just don't know what it is? That's what the Crimson Circle is about." Somehow people just get it. It saves me a lot of anguish and it saves them a lot of tedious explanation.

And, there is something more to life, no matter what your five senses and mind tell you. There is a Beyond and you're not crazy for thinking that there is. You were just trying to find it with your current senses. Once you allow yourself to go beyond your current senses, you'll come to realize that *there is so much more*.

Learn more about the Crimson Circle at www.crimsoncircle.com

    – *Geoffrey Hoppe, channeler for Adamus Saint-Germain*

Other Books
by Geoffrey Hoppe
with Tobias and Adamus Saint-Germain

Act of Consciousness – *Adamus Saint-Germain*

Life is an act. We act like humans, and therefore experience like humans with a litany of limitations, shortcomings and drama that mask our underlying angelic consciousness. It's an unnatural act, but we accept it as reality. However, acting like a Master will literally change the type of energy we attract into our lives, and therefore change the reality in which we exist and experience.

Live Your Divinity – *Adamus Saint-Germain*

A new dimension in spiritual teaching, this intriguing and provocative book will challenge your perceptions of reality, remind you of forgotten truths, and prod you toward the realization and manifestation of your divine nature here on Earth.

Masters in the New Energy – *Adamus Saint-Germain*

This profound and delightful book is filled with insightful and practical information about living as true Masters in the New Energy. Adamus' simple and profound messages provide the guideposts for those who choose to go beyond limited thoughts and beliefs into a new understanding of reality.

Memoirs of a Master – *Adamus Saint-Germain*

A book of short stories that are designed to help you see yourself as both the Master and the student. The student in each memoir is generally a compilation of many people, the Master can be perceived as any enlightened teacher, but ultimately it is you. *Memoirs of a Master* is dedicated to the Master and the student within each of us.

Creator Series – *Tobias*

"*You never go Home. Instead, Home comes to you.*" With these words Tobias laid out an entirely new understanding of how we came to Earth and why this is such an important crossroads on our spiritual journey. The Creator Series is full of practical tools for thriving as an awakening being on Earth.

Other Courses and Additional Material
with Tobias and Adamus Saint-Germain

Tobias' Sexual Energies School

This three-day school focuses on what Tobias calls the "sexual energy virus." It helps the student understand how people energetically feed off of each other, and how to release the chain of the virus. Adamus adds his wisdom, talking about blame, living a powerless life, and true freedom. This is one of the most basic and important courses offered by the Crimson Circle. It is offered online and taught by certified teachers worldwide.

Tobias' Aspectology School

In this three-day workshop, Tobias and Adamus focus on the Aspects or parts of self that negatively affect and sometimes control our lives due to trauma, whether in this or a past life. Learn tools to help you integrate these energies and bring true freedom to your life. This core material is offered online and taught by certified Crimson Circle teachers worldwide.

Tobias' Journey of the Angels School

Hear and see the original presentation by Tobias from which this book was created, given just three weeks before his departure and return to Earth. Weaving together the core of all his teachings over the previous 10 years, *Journey of the Angels* offers a completely different perspective on creation and will radically change your concept of what it really means to be a human.

DreamWalker™ Death Transitions

In this three-day school, offered online and by certified teachers, you learn how to guide friends, family and clients through the death process into the non-physical realms, providing comfort and love to make their transition more peaceful. This School offers certification as a DreamWalker Death Guide.

DreamWalker™ Birth Transitions

This three-day school is offered online and by certified teachers. Saint-Germain defines the birth process from pre-conception and choosing the incoming entity, to post-birth and beyond. Adamus also shares the story of your first birth into biology and the profound implications for your Realization. This School offers certification as a DreamWalker "Adoula" Guide.

DreamWalker™ Ascension Transitions

Adamus Saint-Germain's three day Ascension School provides unique and personal insights into the nature of Ascension, aspect integration, making true choices, and the implications of one's final lifetime on Earth. This course is offered by certified DreamWalker Ascension teachers.

DreamWalker™ Life

This three-day school provides insights on how to truly live in and love life. Through Quantum Allowing and the grace of the crystal flame of transfiguration, attendees learn what it means to be a Master on Earth. Currently offered by certified DreamWalker Life teachers.

New Energy Synchrotize™

Adamus Saint-Germain says Synchrotize goes "beyond hypnosis" for those who want to consciously create their reality. Synchrotize is offered online and by certified teachers. The study process takes four consecutive days to complete.

Standard Technology

Adamus Saint-Germain and Tobias join together to present Standard Technology, a New Energy program for activating your body's natural rejuvenation system. Standard Technology is offered as a Personal Study Course.

The Master's Life (Series)

In this ongoing series of presentations, Adamus Saint-Germain discusses the embodied enlightened life and provides support and inspiration in dealing the challenges of staying here on planet Earth as a Realized Master.

Single and Multi-Session Audio and Video Presentations

Tobias, Adamus and Kuthumi cover a broad range of topics in dozens of recorded presentations. Varying in length from an hour or less to 15 or more hours of channeling, these life-changing sessions are also available with translations in nearly 20 languages.

Monthly Shouds

Text transcripts or audio recordings of all channeled monthly messages since August 1999 are available *free of charge* on the Crimson Circle web site (www.crimsoncircle.com). The Shouds are channeled in annual series (The Creator Series, The New Earth Series, The Divine Human Series, etc.) and also include many Question and Answer sessions. These recordings are an excellent record of Shaumbra's journey since the beginning of the Crimson Circle.

Workshops

Geoffrey and Linda Hoppe present workshops around the world featuring live channelings with Adamus Saint-Germain, Kuthumi and Merlin. Check the Crimson Circle web site for dates and details: www.crimsoncircle.com/Calendar.

*"All you need to do is love yourself,
and you'll understand who you really are."*

- Tobias

Made in the USA
Las Vegas, NV
25 February 2024

86257763R00106